SAFEGUARD

NYC Doms

JANE HENRY

Chapter 1

I hear the clink of metal behind me, and I know I'm in trouble this time. There is no escaping what's going to happen. I'm like a cornered animal with nowhere to go, and the feeling both exhilarates and terrifies me all at once.

"Hands on the wall." His voice, at once sharp and commanding, stops my heart in my chest. Trembling, I do as he says, placing my hands on the wall in front of me. I stare at my small, oval-shaped nails, painted a vibrant crimson, a sharp contrast to the brilliant white wall underneath my hands and for one brief minute, I let myself feel the panic.

He's taking you to prison.

He's going to cuff you, and frisk you, and haul your ass to jail.

I shiver as he approaches me, feeling his presence before I actually see him.

"You knew this would happen," he scolds in a warning tone, the whisper of his voice tickling my skin. "You knew the price you'd pay for breaking the law." A low growl makes a shiver course through me. "Do *not* move those hands." The click of metal against metal reaches my ears, my eyes shut tight as I fully experience my situation, then cold grazes my skin, the slightest warning before my wrists are shackled. I do as he says, frozen in place.

My wrists secured above my head, I brace myself for whatever he'll do next. I'm at his mercy now.

I'm wearing nothing but a thin tank top and shorts despite the chilly fall air, and he makes good use of my bared skin. He begins at my shoulders, strong fingers probing me, slightly painful yet soothing, like a deep tissue massage. He moves over my shoulders, down my back, and a shudder of anticipation weaves its way through me. When he reaches my hips, his hands anchor on either side of me, spanning my taut frame. One hand lifts off my right side and *whack!* With a resounding slap, his palm spanks my ass.

"Such a naughty girl," he says with a cluck of his tongue. "Such wicked things she's done. Things that she knew would get her punished." Even though I can't see him, I can imagine him shaking his head behind me. "What should I do with a bad girl like you?"

I don't answer. It's a rhetorical question. If I speak, he'll punish me. The last time I spoke before he allowed it, he took his belt to my ass. Tonight, I don't know what he's capable of. When he pushed me up against the wall, he had a gleam in his eyes, a look I've learned to both crave and fear.

In silence, I shiver in anticipation. Without warning, he squeezes my ass so hard it hurts, but I only hiss out a breath.

"Very good," he breathes. He shoves his hand between my legs, but doesn't touch where I need him to, his fingers grazing my inner thighs. "I bet we could find a way for you to pay," he says. "To make retribution for breaking the law." A pinch to my ass has me gasping out loud. "Answer me."

"Yes, officer." I bite my lip to keep from smiling. This is my favorite part.

"Do you need to be punished?" he whispers in my ear.

I nod my head vigorously. "I've been wicked. Sinful. Terrible. I need to be taught a lesson."

"Hmm," he says, and he takes his hands off me altogether. "Maybe you need to stand here and think about your transgressions as punishment."

What? No! Wait, wait, wait. What's he talking about?

"Or maybe you need to go to bed without your dinner," he mulls. I turn my head to look at him, growling low enough that he can't hear me, but he catches the vibe. Fuck, he's sexy. He's dressed in his uniform, a black, short-sleeved, button-down shirt, black slacks, and shiny black shoes, complete with a thick leather belt. He doesn't normally wear a uniform but he has one in his closet, and I love when he puts it on for me like this. He's even wearing his badge, which turns me the fuck on.

Officer Zack Williams.

"You're the one who ought to be punished," I say snidely, a lilt of flirtation in my tone. "It's *illegal* to be that sexy." Tattoos sneak under the edges of his shirt, large, muscled shoulders alluding to his strength and power. One corner of his lips quirks up as his golden-brown hair falls across his brow, his chestnut-colored eyes rimmed in stark black lashes meeting mine. He runs a hand across the thick stubble on his jaw.

"I don't think so, sweetheart," he whispers, a wicked note to his voice warning me that shit's about to get very real. "I've only just started with *you.*"

His voice drops, a sharp command like the crack of a

whip. *"Face the wall."* He snaps his fingers, and my spine stiffens. I quickly move to obey. Damn, he's sexy as fuck.

He comes back to me and strips me bare. With a rough tug, my panties and shorts slither to the floor in a puddle leaving me in nothing but my tank. Without a word, he straddles me from behind. I hear the clink of metal and the whir of a zipper. My breath catches. He's going to take me, right here, right now, with my hands cuffed and pushed up against the wall, him fully clothed and me dressed in nothing but a thin tank top.

Squeeeeeeeee.

I barely contain my glee.

"Need to make you submit. Maybe then you'll learn your lesson." He's at my entrance, hard and soft and warm, and fuck, I need him in me. I stopped breathing at the word *submit,* anticipation ringing in my ears. With a savage thrust, he plunges into me with a groan and my breath whooshes out. I gasp for air, inhaling deep, cleansing breaths, grasping the wall for support. He has to bend down so he can take me. I want to brace myself but can't with my wrists bound in cuffs. He's hard, so fucking turned on, and it takes no time at all before he's soaring, grunting his release, and I follow on his tail, a shudder of ecstasy ripping through me. Nothing makes me come harder or faster than when he does this to me.

I sag against the wall, wrists still bound. "I've learned my lesson, officer," I whisper. "I'll be sure to obey the law in the future."

"The fuck you will," he says with a chuckle, giving my ass a playful slap as he withdraws from me. I shiver at the loss, wishing we could've stayed like that for so much longer. But I know him. I know that if I wait, he'll take care of me.

He knows I like losing control, knows I like being taken and used like this.

"I want you to arrest me some time," I whisper. "Will you do that? Like for real with the sirens and cuffs in a cruiser, and then you can punish me for breaking the law like *in the car?*"

"You just don't know where to stop, do you?" he asks. "Next thing I know, you'll want to publicly scene at the club, just ratchet up that fantasy even more? Get a couple of my buddies with their night sticks in on the action?"

"Holy hotness," I breathe. He smacks my ass again, harder this time.

"As if I'd let anyone come anywhere near you but me," he growls in my ear. "Can hardly joke about it. Damn near ready to cuff you to my bed when I leave for work so no one else sees you, touches you. Could beat the shit out of those guys you teach at the gym." He's on his way to my bathroom.

I grin. God, he's so adorable when he gets his alpha on.

"One of them was flirting with me the other day, you know," I say nonchalantly as I hear the water running. "Asked me to dinner."

He comes to the doorway and his body goes tight. "Did he?"

"Yes. But don't worry, honey," I singsong. "I politely told him to screw off."

He moves impossibly closer to me, nearly stifling me. "Babe, would've been okay to tell him so impolitely. Still, you're a good girl," he croons in my ear, cleaning me off. That's Zack. He just fucked me up against the wall and somehow, impossibly, is still a gentleman.

I bite my lip. There's something about *good girl* that undoes me.

5

I never was the good girl. I'm still not. But hearing him say it makes my heart sing a little.

His mouth comes to my ear. "Gonna uncuff you now, baby." I watch as he slides the key in, turns the lock, and my wrists swing free.

He tucks the cuffs neatly into his pocket, then spins me around, pulls me closer, and presses me up against his body. Weaving a hand through my hair, he gently tugs my head back. I look into the chocolate brown of his eyes a split second before he leans down and brushes my lips with his. "Gotta get you to bed," he says. "It's late, and you're teaching a 6 a.m. class tomorrow." He takes me by the hand and leads me to bed.

"Oh, you're no fun," I tease with a pout. "I was hoping we could watch TV. And maybe eat some ice cream or something."

His lips quirk up, but he points to the bed. "Bed, Beatrice."

"But daddy, just two more minutes?" I tease.

He narrows his eyes and points to the bed. "Go get yourself ready and hop in bed."

Teasingly I stick my tongue out, which earns me a good ass smack as I head to the bathroom. I'm really just teasing him. I love that he looks out for me like this. I really *do* want to watch TV and eat junk food, and if he wasn't here, I maybe would. But I know that 5 a.m. wake up in preparation for the early class is seriously not fun on too little sleep, and anything more than a glass of water will make my stomach feel like crap.

Still, it's hard to do this whole adulting thing sometimes.

I brush my teeth and hear him leave the room. I smile with a sudsy mouthful of toothpaste when I look at myself in the mirror. My eyes are cornflower blue, my nose small and pert, lips full and pink. My just-fucked, fine blonde hair is askew, and my cheeks are flushed pink. But most of all, I look *happy*.

I hear my phone beeping in the other room, so I finish washing my face and brushing my hair, then head back to my bed. Zack's sitting on the edge, still dressed in his uniform, with my stack of mail in hand.

"Seriously, Bea, how long has it been since you've gone through this?" he asks, quirking an eyebrow at me.

"Oh, I don't know." I feel a little guilty now. Maybe there's something important in there, but my bills were fine...I think. Still looking at the mail, he distractedly lifts the covers on my bed and pats the sheets for me to get in. I flop face down on the bed, suddenly exhausted, and grab my phone. He asks me something, but I see there's a message from Diana. I swipe to read the text, but before I can, the phone is out of my hand and he's giving me "the look."

"I asked you a question," he says. "Pay attention."

What a lot of people don't know about Zack is that he's more than my *boyfriend*. He's my dom. When he talks to me, he expects I listen.

"What?" I ask.

"I said, did you see this big invitation-looking thing?"

I sit up, curious. "No! What is it?"

He hands me a large ivory envelope with golden accents, the lettering with my name on the front in hand-tooled calligraphy. Whoa. The paper is thick and smooth. I slide a finger underneath the edge as he sorts the junk mail out of the stack, and take out a large, elaborate invitation with a vellum overlay. A name catches my eye. *Chantilly Moore.*

My youngest cousin. It appears Uncle Herb's baby girl is getting married. Immediately, I'm back in my childhood home, the massive, sprawling estate where I grew up, music filtering through the speakers at an outside barbecue with my uncle singing, "Chantilly lace, and a pretty face," while he spins his daughter around. I'm a girl again, sipping a Shirley Temple in stemware, while my cousins and aunts and uncles celebrate my birthday.

I haven't seen Chantilly or Uncle Herb in ten years, since they moved to L.A. A pang of nostalgia hits me in the solar plexus. I swallow hard, then scan the invite.

"My cousin Chantilly's getting married! And she's coming back to New York to do it!"

My heartbeat patters in a rapid beat against my chest.

"*When,* honey?" His voice is patient. "Who knows how long that invitation's been in that pile of mail?"

Oops.

I quickly glance through the small stack of cards in the envelope.

"Shit! The R.S.V.P. card was due two months ago! The wedding's *this weekend.*" My voice catches at the end. Tears spring to my eyes.

"Beatrice," he chides, scolding me. "You can't let this stuff just come in and pile up like this. What if you had something important in here?"

This *was* important.

I wave my hand at him and pull up my phone. "They *were* accepting RSVP's on some website. I know, I *know.* I'll be better about it. Oh, wait. Zack! Tell me you can go?"

He crosses his arms and lifts a brow at me. "When and where?"

I fill him in.

He takes the invitation from my hand and looks it over, then bends down and kisses my temple. "Yeah, baby. Like I'd let you drive all that way alone."

All kinds of happy and scared feelings flutter through

me. I'm taking him *home*. To my *family*. I've fucked the guy ninety ways to Sunday and still haven't told him about my family yet, but the idea of facing them without his protection is nearly unbearable.

"Of course I'll go," he says. "You'll have rules, though."

I shiver with a smile. "Oh?" What kind of rules?"

"We'll talk about that later. For now, see if you can still RSVP. And if you can, put me down for the steak." I punch the RSVP into my phone, send a pleading and apologetic message to Chantilly via the website, then place it down, suddenly exhausted.

I can't miss Chantilly's wedding. But that means letting my parents in on my life again...letting Zack see where I came from, who I was. He'll know I'm not just a yoga teacher in a studio apartment in NYC. He'll meet my parents, and see where I grew up, and... I know what they'll think.

What will *he?*

He tucks the blanket around me, and my eyes feel heavy with sleep.

What we have is good. No, better than good. I don't need things to be... better. Permanent. This is kinda exactly what I like. He has his space, I have mine, and we don't need any of those messy complications like joint bills and his toothbrush near mine, or... *God...* kids.

What we have is perfect.

He doesn't know about my parents... or Carter... or anything. I don't tell anyone. That stuff was all in the *old* Beatrice's life. Not *mine*.

It isn't mine anymore.

Did inviting him just totally fuck things up?

Chapter 2

It's a gorgeous fall night in New York. I shoulder the duffel bag filled with the toys I brought to play with tonight, the clink of metal jingling in my ears, and walk to the gleaming black entrance of Verge.

Some people don't like the crushing crowds of people in NYC, but I live for it. I grew up on the East Coast, a little place called Cape Cod, south of Boston, right on the water. My mom and dad were steady church-goers, and we owned a tiny, split-level ranch just a few blocks from the ocean. I'd go there on my bike after I'd delivered papers on my paper route, taking in the crash of the waves on the shore, the cry of the gulls, inhaling the salty sea air. I liked knowing that the ocean in front of me stretched further than I could see, touching the coasts of different countries, different lives, connected somehow beyond my own small world. I always thought I'd stay local, by the shore and the ocean. I never imagined I'd move to the city.

Then tragedy struck. When Alicia died, I had a driving force to be that person who protected others, who tracked down the lawbreakers and slammed their asses into jail. So I pursued a career in law enforcement. I started in Boston and transferred to NYPD several years later. There was nothing like the adrenaline rush of an inner-city NYPD job to feed my need for control, order, and justice, my skills at piecing things together with skill leading me to become a detective.

I open the door to Verge, and Brax stands in the entryway, looking down on me. Massively tall, sarcastic as hell, and intimidating as a bouncer with his arms crossed and feet planted in heavy boots, he smirks at me. "Lady friend dump your ass?" he asks, with a shake of his shaved head. "Find out you were too straight-laced for her after all? Dude, you should've pretended to like threesomes."

I smirk. Wiseass. "Yeah, no." I push past him. We go way back, and I've known him since the founding of Verge. He loves to give me shit and is particularly on my ass because I actually have a steady girl here for once. "She had some girl thing to do with Diana, so she's coming in with Diana and Tobias tonight."

Brax grins. "I know. Tobias told me earlier. Just givin' you shit."

I play-punch him in the abs and he jumps back with an "*oof*."

"Everything kosher tonight?" I have no reason to believe anything's out of place, but I still have to ask. I can't *not* ask. I need to know.

He nods, and I move past him. He's right though. It is weird to be here without Beatrice. And I have stuff I need to talk to her about tonight, so I hope she isn't late. I also have a treat for her in my bag, and my dick's getting hard just thinking about it. She's gonna go crazy. I can't wait to see her eyes light up like a summer day, blue and sparkling with excitement when I show her. First, though, she has to be a good girl and do what she's told.

I make my way past the lobby and enter the main bar area of Verge. Even though I'm here tonight as a member and not on the job, I can't help but do my instinctive quick scan around the room. I note that all exits are unimpeded, in case of emergency. The lighting is bright, and there's no one whose eyes look guiltily at me, no eyes shifting suspiciously. They know who I am, and even though I don't wear a badge or uniform, they snap to attention when I walk in.

And fuck me, I like that.

"Hey, man," Travis greets with an amicable fist bump as I near the bar. He's a good kid, just graduated college last spring and is now looking for a full-time job. Tobias and Seth, Verge club owners, pay him well, though, and he's making his way here. Originally from the south, his drawl colors his speech, which somehow makes the ladies go all googly-eyed for him. Or maybe it's his sandy-brown hair, keen blue eyes, and muscular frame. He's sporting a new beard I haven't seen on him before. He's a good guy, the best there is, and I like him a lot. Though he's young, he's easily as mature as most guys I know a decade older.

"What's up, man," I greet, pulling out a stool. I set my bag down next to me and he smirks.

"Got something good in there tonight?" he asks, pulling me a Sam Adams on tap without even asking me. He slides the cool, frothy beer over to me and I take a long, refreshing pull before I answer. I exhale, feeling a little bit of the weight of the day leaving me as I settle into the familiarity of friends, a second home, and my favorite drink.

I smirk. "Maybe." He knows I'm a vault. He'll get shit all as far as details from me.

He grins. "C'mon, man. I haven't gotten to play in the dungeon in a week, and I'm jonesin' to scene. Let a brother live vicariously through you?"

"Not on your life, douchebag."

He shakes his head, reaches under the counter, and pushes over a small, round bowl of warmed mixed nuts. I take an almond and crunch it between my teeth, chasing it with beer. God, it feels good to be here. It's my routine: strip out of my work clothes, hit the gym. Shower, go see Beatrice and bring her here, or take her somewhere else. I missed seeing her today and feel a little antsy. I need her here with me.

"Fine," he says, leaning back against the bar and crossing his arms during a momentary lull. "Fair enough. Anything going on interesting at work?"

He knows I'm a detective for the NYPD and I can't usually discuss things, but some days I can give him basic facts.

"Yeah, man," I say. "Today was a good one, actually. Caught the asshole who's been ripping off credit cards in College Coffee all week." College Coffee is a stone's throw from Verge, and one of the most popular coffee shops for college students in NYC, because they cater to students: a library, reference room, station to charge laptops and phones, and cheap but good coffee, they're a local student hangout. I was pissed when it came to my attention someone was ripping off credit cards, and happy to find the perpetrator.

"Can't tell you who the guy was, but let's just say don't always trust your professors, Trav."

He shakes his head. "No shit. Did I ever tell you about my French teacher who tried to seduce me?"

I slug back another long gulp of cold beer, wipe my mouth with a napkin, and shake my head. "No, man."

"She was a married woman with three grown kids, old enough to be my mother. But shit if she wasn't a knockout."

I grin at him. "And you said no?"

"Course I did," he says, shaking his head, pulling another drink for someone else. "Did you miss the part where I said married woman?"

I smirk. "Don't blame you."

"Speaking of illegal," comes a beautiful, lilting voice behind me. "Coming in here looking like that ought to be *illegal.*" I turn around on my stool, see the familiar halo of blonde hair. I toss my arm around her waist, and pull her onto my knee, wrapping my hand around the back of her neck and giving her a kiss.

"You're the one half dressed," I growl in her ear. "What the *fuck* are you wearing?"

She's got these skin-tight pants and a small, lavender-colored top on. She smiles at me, perched on my knee. "I ended up covering for a class at the gym and barely made it in time to get to check out the venue with Diana. Haven't had a chance to change, but I will. I just needed to see you first."

"You didn't tell me you had a change of plans," I told her, not happy with this. I like to know where she is, when she's leaving, and who she's with. Some would say it's controlling, but she's my submissive and this isn't some small-town suburb, but NYC.

"Oh," she says with a frown, then a grimace. "I forgot."

"You forgot." I fix her with a stern glare. I consider punishing her. She loves to play but I have real rules and she knows better than this. I'm watching her response, making sure that she's doing what she's supposed to.

Her shoulders sag. "I'm sorry, sir," she says, and she really does look repentant.

"Good. Go get dressed. Come back here when you're finished. I'm taking you to the dungeon tonight, and we need to go over things first."

She smiles at me, leans in, and kisses my cheek. "Yes, sir." She quickly skips away to obey. Shit, I love when she calls me *sir,* most definitely not something that comes naturally to her. But it's what she does as my submissive. She needs this. I won't have it any other way.

After she's gone, and I turn back to my beer. Travis is watching me curiously. "You make her tell you where she is?"

"Always."

He nods thoughtfully. "Some girls would find that overbearing you know."

I shrug. "Good thing I'm not dating some girl. Some girls would find *me* overbearing. Some wouldn't like being bent over my knee, or strapped to the St. Andrew's cross, but what can I say? She likes it." And if that isn't the understatement of the year. She fucking craves it. I need more, though. It's time I kick things up a notch with her. But not without her permission.

I keep an eye on the door that will bring her back to me after she's changed, needing to see her, my eyes roaming the interior, when my friends Tobias and Diana appear in the doorway. Diana's eyes light up when she sees me, and Tobias gives me a chin lift.

"Hey!" Diana greets, holding Tobias's hand as they approach. "We were hoping to find you here tonight." Tobias clears his throat and slides into a bar stool, guiding Diana into the one next to him. I can tell they're a little nervous or excited about something, and I'm curious what. I polish off my beer and push the mug over to Travis.

"So, you know the wedding's coming up," Tobias begins. Tobias is a big guy, strong and serious, with swarthy skin and dark hair that falls onto his forehead. He's part-owner of Verge, Beatrice's best friend Diana's fiancé.

"Yeah?" Tobias proposed to Diana six months ago.

"We're wondering if you'd be my best man," Tobias asks. I blink in surprise. I expected he'd ask his friend Seth, his partner. They've known each other longer, though we're all tight.

"Yeah, man, I'd be honored," I say, and Tobias grins. I give him a man hug, the kind where I lean over and smack his back hard enough to hurt.

"Seth's traveling," Diana explains. She entwines her fingers through Tobias' as she fills me in. She is taller than Beatrice, with a mane of dark, unruly curls and wide, hazel eyes. "He and Rochelle are spending a month overseas, and they can't change plans. And seeing as Beatrice is my maid of honor, we really would love it if you'd escort her as the best man."

"Of course," I say.

"You don't feel, like, second fiddle, right?" Beatrice's pretty voice comes from behind me.

"Of course not," I say, turning to her. "Guys don't think of shit like—"

But I freeze when I see her and somehow lose the ability to speak. She's wearing all leather, a sleeveless dress that zippers up the front and ends at the very top of her thighs, revealing her shapely legs. Her hair's in some kind of crazy spring thing, the blonde tresses as pretty as a picture, wispy and fetching, making her look way too innocent, belying the inner vixen I know all too well.

"What the *fuck* are you wearing?" I ask, pushing myself to my feet.

Her eyes go quickly to Diana who merely shrugs. "I

wash my hands of this," she says. "You know I told you you'd get your ass whipped for that outfit."

"Oh, she will," I say in a growl, but I'm fucking hard as hell and can't wait to push that dress up and take her. "Which, I think, is *exactly* what she wanted."

Her eyes gleam and she bites her lip. "Who, me?" she asks.

The room fades for a moment and all I see is her, on her knees, the two of us alone. She wants this. I *need* this. Without conscious thought, I snap my fingers and she drops to the floor, both knees hitting the floor simultaneously, but maintaining eye contact. Other doms demand their subs look at the floor, but I've taught her not to break contact with me. I need to see her eyes, need to read her.

Still keeping her eyes on mine, I kneel in front of her on one knee and grab the bag I brought.

"It was on special," she whispers. "At the bridal shop."

"You bought that thing at the *bridal* shop?"

She smiles. "It's NYC, sir. They have a goth line."

I pull out the surprise I brought for her and hold it in my palm. I give her a quick nod, my cue to her giving her permission to break eye contact and look at what I'm holding. It's a beautiful, handcrafted leather collar.

"For tonight?" I ask her. It isn't a permanent one but a play one, sturdy, though, and fitted with rings so I can attach the chain. She has a fetish for depravity and craves being objectified. I can only take it so far. But a collar and chain? Yeah, I'm down with that.

"Zack," she breathes. "Oh, it's beautiful."

I turn it around so she can see what I had stamped on the black leather. *Good girl.* Turning to face her, I slide the collar on her neck and click it into place. "Be my good girl tonight?" I ask her.

She nods, but only slightly, as she's staying still for me

to fasten it. After it's secured, I reach into my bag and take out the thin, supple steel chain, and fasten it onto the ring on her neck. "Back on your feet, doll," I say quietly. "You'll wear my collar tonight, but not on your knees. Walk with me."

She stands, her eyes bright, lips parted. If I reach my hands between her legs, I'll find her soaked. She loves this and knowing that makes me hard as fuck for her.

"Later, kids," I say to Tobias and Diana. Tobias gives us a chin lift and a smirk, and Diana smiles brightly.

"Be good, Bea," she calls. "I saw some other things lurking in that bag."

Tobias slaps her thigh, but she only laughs.

We aren't the only couple here with a collar and chain. It's common in a BDSM club like Verge for submissives, bottoms, and slaves to wear collars and chains, but tonight, I feel like royalty while I'm walking through the room, my girl under my command like this. I take her to the violet room, the one I've reserved for us tonight. As a long-term member I'm given the privilege of a private room like this whenever I want, and tonight, this is what I want. It irks me she hasn't come to my place yet—won't do it and I don't know why. But at least I like being able to get a drink first, and to sample the many accoutrements Verge has to offer if I want to.

Tonight, I want her eventually alone. The private room is a compromise. In my bag I have a leather strap, a lexan paddle, a rubber paddle, a pair of clamps, and a few other things she hasn't yet sampled.

I hold her chain in my hand and lead her to the side of the entryway door, leaning in to whisper in her ear. "You gonna be my pain slut tonight, sweetheart?"

She nods eagerly, eyes bright. "Yes, sir."

"Good girl." She closes her eyes briefly. There's something about *good girl* that she loves. I open the door and tug her in behind me, and then shut and lock the door. Tonight, Beatrice is all mine.

Chapter 3

Holy mother of the hottest things in the *world,* he's not doing this. But he is! He's never taken me to this room, never outfitted me in a chain, and definitely never put a collar around my neck. Though I know it's temporary, I love it, I crave it, and I'm already primed for him. I can feel the arousal pulsing between my thighs, my nipples taut against the tight dress.

"Gonna spank your ass for wearing that dress," he says, shutting the door behind me with an audible click. "You need your ass whipped for that."

"Yes, sir," I say. *Fuck yes.*

He tosses his bag on the floor and snaps his fingers, pointing to the small square of carpet in front of a large, overstuffed chair. When he sits, I fall between his knees, kneeling, my ass on my heels as he's trained me, and I stare into his beautiful, provoking eyes. He cups my cheek in his hand, and I can tell by the look in his eyes something troubles him, but when he has me like this he wants me listening, not asking questions. When he brushes a thumb across the apple of my cheek, my eyes flutter closed. His hand is warm, the pads of his thumb calloused. He touches me as if he owns me. In Verge, he does.

"You're beautiful, Beatrice." I open my eyes and want to say, *and you are, too,* but I keep quiet. It isn't easy for me to obey someone and every single time he doms me, I fight it. It's winning the victory that makes me come back for more. "Turn around and present yourself to me."

I'm familiar with this pose. Presentation is like the *child's pose* yoga move I teach my students at the gym, my chest and belly down, ass in the air, and when I'm with him, arms stretched straight out on the floor in front of me. Sometimes he makes me strip and present. Sometimes I present on the bed and wait for a spanking. This is the first time he's ever made me present on the floor. They keep it immaculately clean in here, though, and the violet room is carpeted in clean black carpet. The cool floor beckons me to prostate myself, welcoming my submission to Zack.

While I'm like this, the edge of my skirt pulls up so high that I feel the breath of air across my panty-clad ass. I close my eyes. This, to me, is fucking *bliss.* I need him to use me. I crave it.

His hand comes to the edge of my dress, his palm so large he practically covers my whole ass. "Fucking beautiful," he approves, before he lifts his hand and *smack!* He spanks me, hard. He gives me another smack, then another, priming my ass for what I can guarantee will be a helluva lot more than this. He reaches into the bag, I hear a whisper of fabric, and then something light and silky caresses my forehead. His blindfold shuts out the light behind my lids, then I feel him secure it behind the back of my head. With my sigh now gone, by other senses heighten, the smell of polished wood in the room, the dimmed sound of voices and laughter down the hall, the tingle of anticipation along my skin.

Yes.

"You like this, doll?" he asks.

"Yes, sir."

He's kneeling behind me as he adjusts my blindfold, then he whispers in my ear. "You trust me, then, Beatrice. It's a gift you give me, that trust. You know that?"

I nod, suddenly choked with emotion. It is. I do trust him. But I need him to exploit me. It's the only way I'll earn his attention. I'm not worthy of a man like him.

He slaps my ass again and I take it, needing more, needing harder.

"Question for you, Bea, before we play. Did you do what was on your list today?"

Oh. *Shit.* My list? We talked about this last night and I completely forgot.

"Um… well."

Smack.

"No, sir!"

He sighs, and he's not playing now, but serious. "I gave you instructions today," he corrects. I hear him reach into his bag. "You're getting spanked for that, you know."

Damn. My stomach drops to my toes and I'm both turned on and a little sad that I'm not just being spanked but punished.

"What were you supposed to do?"

I cringe, but don't move my arms, my eyes still closed behind the blindfold.

"Pay my credit card bill, sir."

Now I'm not only getting slapped with a fine, I'm getting slapped with whatever Zack has in that bag of his.

"Six strokes of the cane, young lady."

Oh, *fuck*. I hear him reach into his bag and I begin to tremble. The cane is *wicked*.

I've only been caned once, and it was months ago, the night that I forgot to tell him I was home after a night out with friends. I'd fallen asleep in a margarita-induced haze, and the next morning woken up to a Zack pounding on my door, followed by a caning I'd never forget.

My body tenses, waiting for the first wicked cut. The only warning I get is the *swish* through the air right before it lands. I cringe, hardly able to bear the fiery lick of fire across my ass. He doesn't even need to swing hard, the cane is that severe.

A second lick of the cane follows the first. He pauses several agonizing seconds between strokes, then lands one after the other. I can feel the thin lines of welts crisscrossing my ass. I'm holding my breath, waiting for the sixth and final wicked cut. It blazes across my ass. I slump, and the tension leaves my body.

He caresses my welted skin, his tone softer now. "I don't like punishing you, Bea." My blindfold is wet with tears. This isn't what I expected tonight. But somehow, oddly, crazily, I *need* this. The accountability. The discipline.

And hell if the serious shit doesn't turn me *on*.

"You took that well," he says in my ear, a purr that soothes my tears. "Crawl back over to me, now, sweetheart." Still blindfolded, I follow the tug of his chain, facing him. I hear a zip and a whir. Excitement builds in my belly, my lady parts zinging to life when I realize what he's about to do. Totally subdued by the caning, he's going to make me suck him off. I can't breathe for the anticipation.

I feel my hair being tugged, pulled back hard. I shake with arousal, so fucking turned on I squeeze my legs together as I go to him on my knees and he draws me closer, fist in my hair. "Such a dirty girl. If I touch you, will I find you wet?"

I nod eagerly though my voice wavers. "Yes, sir."

"I should punish you again for getting turned on from your punishment." He's teasing me and turning me on even more. "Haven't used the whipping post yet, and I could find some other ways to punish you, too. You gonna show me how sorry you are?"

I nod my head eagerly, my fisted hair tugging in his hand. He pats my cheek with his fingers, not hard enough to slap but firm enough it's sobering. His voice drops to a harsh command. "*Open.*"

I obey, opening my mouth eagerly, ready to show him I'll obey.

I LAY on the bed next to him. We can't hear anything outside the door of our private room, and it almost feels like we've got the place to ourselves, but somehow the knowledge that other couples mingle right beyond our door makes what just happened so much hotter. I feel half-drugged, having climaxed four times and been spanked soundly, my eyes are beginning to close.

Zack gives *the best* fucking aftercare *ever.* He held me on his lap and stroked my hair, let me nuzzle my head against the hollow of his neck while he whispered sweet, soothing words, telling me how proud he was of me, and how he'll help me be a good girl.

He wants me to go to his place. But somehow, it's safer here. What we do here is a scene.

We can sleep here tonight if we want to. As a gold status member, Zack had the privilege of using the private room at will, and we keep some things here for overnight stays. I roll over and flop my arm across the expanse of his body, the little hairs scattered across his chest tickling my arm. He loops an arm around me and pulls me closer.

"Before you fall asleep," he says, his voice stern. "What are you gonna do tomorrow?"

"You mean today?" I tease, my lips quirking. It's well after midnight.

He slaps my ass playfully, and it hurts like hell after being spanked earlier. "Ouch! Ok, ok, yes, I'll pay my credit card before I pack for us to go." I don't want to talk about it. I close my eyes and hold him tighter. The wedding's this weekend, and I have mixed feelings. A weekend away with Zack? Hell yeah. Time spent with my family? Not so much.

"I've already packed, and my bag's in your closet at your place," he says. "Thought it would be easier since we're leaving from there in the morning."

"How'd I end up in bed with a Boy Scout?" I mumble. "I barely remember to pay my bills." But I'm not really complaining. I've dated losers, and I've dated good guys, and the good guys win, hands down. But I like teasing him.

"Pretty sure I carried you to bed tonight," he says, huffing out a laugh. He did. I was boneless after he'd had his way with me, and we'd never even made it to the bed. Tonight, when he was done, he lifted me up and tucked me under the covers on the bed. I swallow up his sweetness like a cat laps milk.

"Thassrite," I slur. "Something like that. Can we talk about the responsible adult things tomorrow?"

A jingling sound makes him freeze. Shit. It's his call line, the important one he can't ignore when they come in. He has to take it. *Shit shit shit.* A Boy Scout with a job to do. Sigh.

He releases me, pushes out of the bed, and trots to the phone, swipes it on and puts it up to his ear.

"Williams." He pauses and listens. "No *shit*. The fucker. Yeah, of course. Keep me posted." He shuts it off, his jaw clenched.

"What's up, honey?"

"Closing in on a suspect," he says, coming back to bed. "Flint's got it tonight and will let me know if anything comes up."

Technically, he's off duty, and it's the only reason why we're at Verge. He wouldn't make plans for us here if he wasn't. But I know the truth after dating him for half a year. He's never really *off duty*, just like he never really *sleeps*. It's who he is. He can't settle when there's someone out there threatening to harm someone else.

"Zack, *go* honey. I'm fine. Tobias and Diana are here, and I can hitch a ride home with them."

"Nah, it's good," he says, but when he joins me in bed again, he's tense, alert. I can feel his heart pounding under my palm when I place my arm around him. Something big's about to go down, and he can't tell me details, but he isn't here anymore. His mind is somewhere else. I take a deep breath in.

"Let's go back to my place," I say. "I really would feel better because then I can get up early and pack, and if you need to go, you can take off."

"Yeah?"

"Yeah," I say. "C'mon. I'm fine." I shake off the exhaustion from a moment before and sit up in bed. I stifle a yawn. I don't want him to know how badly I want to stay.

We quickly pack our things and go to his cruiser parked in the back lot of Verge. There are only three spaces in the congested city lot, one for the Club owners and the other they give to Zack.

I love driving in his car, a small black coupe that easily blends into the crowded city streets. He's got all sorts of buttons and flashy lights and things inside the car, but I'm not allowed to touch anything. Still, I like to tease.

"If I push this one here, will it eject me?" I ask, my finger hovering over a small, oval-shaped button on his dash, lit up with fluorescent green.

"Beatrice," he warns.

"Or this one?" I asked, hovering now over the speaker where he communicates with dispatch when he needs to. I know he's also tricked out with sirens and lights, and there's something exhilarating about riding in his car.

"Beatrice *Ann*," he warns. My heart kicks up in my chest, my ass still burning from the punishment I got earlier in the club. "So soon you forget how it feels to have my palm across your ass?"

Jesus, I'm getting turned on again.

"Just teasing you," I say with a mock pout, when we slow at a light. Suddenly, his eyes brighten, and his body stiffens. The light turns green, and he curses vehemently. "*Son of a bitch.*" Before I know what's happening, he flicks a button and flashing lights surround us. It takes a second before I realize the lights are from the car *he's* driving, and the deafening screech of a siren is coming from *us*.

Oh my God! We're going after a bad guy! Or girl. Whatever.

I grip the dash and look to him, my mouth parted in expectation. He's never driven with me on a chase before like this.

"What is it? What happened?"

"Shh," he says, flicking something on his phone and growling into the mouthpiece. "Found the asshole. He's three cars up, but I caught a good glimpse at him. He's our suspect. Back up to Lafell!" He switches off the speaker and accelerates, cursing under his breath. "Wish I'd left you at Verge. *Sonofabitch*. This wasn't supposed to happen now. *Jesus*. Flint had 'em." He swerves in and out of traffic easily. "I have to get you to safety."

"I'm fine," I say, which just elicits another growl. "For God's sake, Zack, chill."

"Chill?" he snaps. "I'm tailing the most infamous drug lord since 1997 with my girlfriend in my cruiser, and you're telling me to chill?"

I get a clue and close my mouth. The man doesn't like when I forget to floss, for crying out loud. Putting me in danger while on the job is akin to drowning puppies or something. Better to just keep my mouth shut and let him do his thing and enjoy the ride. I can't wait to tell Diana about this when I get home. I have to bite my lip to keep from hollering out loud at him to go get the bad guys.

In my head, I'm cheering him on.

It's cool how cars part for us, moving out of our way at the sight of flashing lights and deafening sirens. In NYC it's not uncommon for people to push in front of you no matter who you are, so it's super cool to see how they get out of our way. My heart smacks against my rib cage as he takes a left on what feels like two wheels, the siren blaring as we pursue the silver car that's easily going as fast as we are. I feel like I'm on the set of a TV show while our tires whir beneath us, adrenaline pumping. Hell, I can almost hear the thundering beat of a theme song.

The car we're chasing is fast, but Zack's is made for speed, and the other guy can't match Zack's city driving prowess. Zack easily navigates in and out of lanes, swerving to avoid parked cars, and the silver car he's tailing plows ahead like a linebacker, razing everything in its path, but that's a shitty way to drive in the city. A rearview mirror snaps off on the driver's side and whips past my window and suddenly I hear a pop and see smoke, can smell rubber burning as one tire rips open, and the silver car comes stuttering to a halt. Before the car stops, the doors open, and Zack's already slamming his breaks.

"Fucking get *down*," he says to me, pulling out his handgun out of his holster, and shoving the door open. "You do not move!"

And he's gone. My heart thunders in my chest now. I loved the pursuit, but my man just left the car to take on a wanted criminal by himself. I actually toy with the idea of getting out, not doing what he said, and helping him in… some way. But what the fuck am I going to do? Smack someone with my heel? And even if I *did* rescue him or… something… he'd whip my ass for getting out of the car to begin with. Yeah, not smart.

I pout a little, tucking myself down below the dash as he said. This isn't exactly what a human is supposed to do in this part of the car, and it's uncomfortable as hell and smells like feet.

Fun times, dating a cop.

I squeeze my eyes shut, praying Zack is safe, that someone hasn't hurt him. A blast of shots ring out and I cringe. Fuck, I need to see what's going *on*. I whisper vehement prayers and hold my breath, when the sound of a door wrenching open startles me. A short, stocky bald man with a scar that runs the length of his face from temple to chin, grins wickedly at me.

"Thought so," he says in a sinister whisper. "Got your man down, and I swear I thought I saw somethin' pretty behind the dash. Come here, baby." He reaches for me and instinctively, I react. I grab his wrist and bite his hand, hard, my teeth sinking into his chubby fingers. I want to vomit at the taste but take grim satisfaction in the howl of pain and vicious string of curse words he utters. He barely recovers when he's leaning in, and he yanks me by the hair so viciously I screech from the pain. He hauls me out of the car and shoves me against the door, and lifts his hand to slap me, but something dark slams into him from behind. I blink, startled.

Zack's come for me. He smacks the handle of his gun into the guy's temple, and the man crumples to the ground.

Zack steps over the man's body and grabs me, yanking me close to him. "You alright? Fuck, what a shitshow."

Though my heart is still hammering in my chest, I grin at him. "I'm fine. Are *you* ok?" I look to the side and see three cruisers and two men being cuffed.

"Yeah," he says, running a hand through his hair. "Glad I got here in time, though. Shit."

I huff out a laugh. "I so totally could've defended myself!"

"He had you by the hair," he says, and the humor flees from his face. He scowls at the man at his feet, bends down, and snaps a pair of cuffs on his wrists, and I can tell he wants to do a helluva lot more than cuff the man.

"You pulled my hair earlier," I say coyly, hoping to lighten the situation.

He raises a brow and shakes his head, but one corner of his lips arches up.

After his friends have taken away the men Zack hunted down, we go back to my place. I'm exhausted, and we leave first thing in the morning for my cousin's wedding. I collapse into bed after stripping out of my clothes and doing the bare minimum nighttime routine.

"Sorry you had to see all that," Zack says, standing in the doorway to the bathroom holding his toothbrush. "I hate that you were with me tonight." He starts brushing his teeth, and his next sentence is garbled. "Would've fuckin' killed the bashtards."

"I know you would have, honey," I say, sighing, still feeling the burn of my spanked ass, my heart still pumping at the memory of the night we've had. "But I didn't hook up with, like, an accountant or something. Cop stuff is messy."

He snorts, goes back into the bathroom, and rinses his mouth. "True."

I groan inwardly when I remember what we have to do tomorrow. "And honey? You pursuing drug lords or whatever the fuck might look tame compared to what you'll be facing tomorrow."

"That bad?"

I groan. "You have no idea."

Chapter 4

The sky is still dark, the sun not yet risen, when I gently wake Beatrice. To say she's not a morning person is the understatement of the year.

"Two more minutes," she mumbles, not even moving. I give her ass a teasing smack.

"No time for two more minutes, babe. You move now, and we have time for you to pack and grab coffee before we hit the road. We wait much longer we'll hit rush hour and that'll make me grumpy."

"Waking up early makes me grumpy," she says, her eyes still shut tight.

"Beatrice," I warn.

She mumbles something incoherent.

I shake my head, push out of bed, and take a quick shower. "When I get out of this bathroom, you'd better be up." I come back a few minutes later, and she's still dead asleep. She hears the noise, though, and bolts upright, her eyes flying open.

"I'm awake, I'm awake."

I stifle a chuckle. Damn, this girl pushes my buttons.

She shoves things in bags at a crazy speed when I go back to finish up in the bathroom, and I swear she's taking her whole fucking closet. After trimming my beard, I come out and stare at the pile of bags she's got lined up.

"Really? Blue and pink, eh? Is this, like, some kinda statement?" I hold her bag up and frown. It's like a tropical plant on steroids. She's got three more just like it.

She yawns widely, stretched her arms up over her head, and mutters. "Excuse me, male person, it is fuchsia and teal, and the latest rage. That bag you're mocking cost more than my rent this month and lucky for me, one of my clients works at Breedell and got me a deal." She bends down to pick up a stray pair of heels and throws them back in her closet.

I take off my towel, roll it up, and snap it at her naked ass. She squeals and runs to the bathroom.

I yell through the bathroom door. "Bea. Seriously, babe. We're going for *four days*. You need three bags, a purse that looks like I could legit fit your refrigerator in it if I needed to, some kind of a... something with like this latch that jingles."

"Makeup bag!" she yells through the door, her voice muffled from the stream of water.

I open the door to the bathroom. "You wear makeup?"

"Is that a real question, or rhetorical?" she asks. I can see her soaping her legs through the clouded glass, and my dick grows hard. But fuck, we don't have time.

"Real. I mean I know I've seen you put on like lip gloss or something..."

"Zack. I'm a girl. Girls wear makeup when it comes to weddings. I don't wear it every day, but for weddings, I have to pull out *all the stops*. Honey. *All. The Stops.*"

Yeah, now I'm definitely hard.

"Yeah?" I ask, sliding the shower door open. Her

blonde hair is piled on top of her head and slathered in some sorta cream, a trail of bubbles adorably skittering down her shoulder, razor poised over her leg.

"Uh uh," she says, waving her razor at me. "Out you go. We do not have time for hanky panky!"

I snort. "You're such a dork. And if I want to fuck you before we go, that's a dom's prerogative."

She purses her lips, inhales, then exhales, her eyes shining. "Yes, sir."

"Mmm," I say, closing the shower door. "I like when you say that." She knows I do, and it's exactly why she's saying it now.

"God almighty, it's like a fucking sauna in here," I say, hardly able to breathe. "And seriously. You need *all* those bags. For *four days?* Like, how many pairs of shoes are you bringing?"

"Six!" she says, as I shut the door to the bathroom. I have one sister... well, one now. And Tia is a total tomboy. She wears practical jeans, no jewelry, and hates makeup. We used to camp when we were kids, and we wore the same hoodies and sweats for a week. I do not get this high-maintenance thing.

After packing the car, a considerable feat, we take off, only five minutes behind schedule. I've never been on a road trip with Beatrice before. She belts out music, her feet on the dash, uninhibited once the coffee kicks in. We talk about anything and everything. She chatters and asks questions, makes me laugh and cringe and wanna smack her ass.

"So," I say, when we finally reach the last stretch of road that will take me to her parents' house. "Why are you dreading this so much?"

She sobers and looks away. "Don't want to talk about it."

"Yeah, well, you don't have much of a choice. We're heading to your parents' house and I want some kinda heads up, babe. You're kinda out of evasion time."

She sighs. "So. My parents are… filthy rich."

I chuckle. "Well, that's not a bad thing."

"Um, yes, it is," she says. "You have no idea, Zack. They're gonna be so fucking hoity toity at this wedding I might disown them."

"Is that all? So they're rich and snobby?" She looks out the window and shrugs.

"*Beatrice.*"

She sighs. "They want me to marry this guy I grew up with. Judson Tolstoy Hayes."

"*Judson Tolstoy?*"

"Yep. His parents were, like, literature professors at some Ivy League school."

"Just… wow. I feel so *pleb* all of a sudden."

She giggles. "Tell me about it. Though you know my name is also literary?"

"Yeah?"

"Mhm. Beatrice is a snarky main character in a Shakespeare play?"

"Right." Damn. I already feel out of my element and I haven't even met her parents yet.

"So, tell me about this guy."

She groans. "He's a pompous jackass, but when we were in third grade, I kissed him." I smirk. "Third graders do stupid shit, but our parents were insistent it was some sort of premonition or something. They had this grand idea that the businesses would merge, families would become one, and we'd all live happily ever after."

I don't respond, focusing my eyes on the road. I do not like the fact I'm walking into this with her.

"So what happened?"

She shifts a little, pursing her lips, and finally blows out a breath. "I dated him, briefly, in high school, but it was only to appease my parents. I resisted every advance he's made on me since then, and wish he'd leave me the fuck alone."

"Wait. Leave you alone? You mean you're still in contact?"

She looks back out the window and shrugs. "You know, Facebook and stuff."

I do *not* like this. "I see."

"And he's so excited I'm coming to the wedding, and I couldn't be *less* excited about seeing him *or* my parents again, but it's Chantilly's wedding, and I can't miss that for *anything.*"

The plot thickens and I'm not too thrilled. "Ok, then. So... do your parents know you brought a guest?"

She cringes, her eyes apologetic. "I may have... neglected to mention that."

"But didn't you RSVP?"

She shrugs. "Well, yes, but... remember I was late? Chantilly manually added me, and I didn't want to push things, so what's one more?"

I frown. I don't like this at all.

"I'm not ashamed of you, Zack," she says, which somehow verbalizes shit I don't want to hear. "I just couldn't deal with my parents and knew that when they saw you, they'd see why I'm with you."

I can't help but chuckle. "Nice save." She's in a hard situation, and I can't blame her. The truth is, I hide shit from my parents, too. "Yeah, I get what it's like, sorta," I say. "I mean, my parents live in a residence home south of Boston, on the Cape. They play cribbage and volunteer at the food pantry. They're proud of Zachary the cop, but they would be appalled at Zack the Dom."

She giggles. "If my parents had any idea…"

Now that we're out of the city, the road widens, and is lined with huge maples, turning red and gold and chestnut. The autumn wind kicks up, wind whipping in the opened windows as we drive. For the first time since we set off, we're seeing residential homes line the streets, as big as football stadiums. They're magnificent. This isn't anything I'm familiar with at all.

"Almost there," she whispers, "God, I want to turn around and go back home." Her voice wavers, and whatever doubt I had about her parents flees with the sudden knowledge that I need to take care of her.

"It's gonna be okay," I say to her, but I don't know if it's me or her I'm speaking to.

We drive in silence for a time until the GPS says we're only a short distance away. She grows visibly nervous, wiping her hands on her pants. "I don't want to do this," she whispers. I look at her in surprise. Beatrice is not a wallflower, not easily cowed by any stretch. Just last week, the bouncer at Verge got on the case of a girl Bea knew from work, and I had to practically pull her off a guy twice her size. She's a spitfire, this one. I don't like that she's subdued like this even if I'm dreading going to her family's goddamn home. I grew up with the white picket fence and Friday night pizza. We watched TV and camped in the summer and my mom canned her own veggies and preserves. My life was simple, and homey, and comfortable.

At least until the summer of my senior in high school… But I still remembered times my mom had gotten food stamps, and the hand-me-downs we used to get from the rummage sale at the little church we frequented.

"So when was the last time you heard from this Judson guy?"

She sighs and bites her lip but doesn't respond at first. That's weird.

"Bea?"

"Welllll…"

I feel my stomach clench and I grip the steering wheel a little harder.

"Beatrice Ann."

"Oh, I hate when you pull out the middle name," she sighs. "Um. Last I heard from him was last night. He Face-booked me."

An unpleasant prickle of cold trickles down my neck. "Was that before or after I fucked you?"

She winces, and I immediately regret the snap. God, what the fuck is my problem?

"Zack," she whispers, a plea.

I huff out a breath. "Sorry, babe," I say, reaching for her knee. "I'm kinda keyed up about all this. That wasn't cool."

"Hard to answer anyway," she said. "Considering we fucked at the club and then when we got home." She's teasing me, but her voice is tremulous. Jesus, I'm an asshole.

Her fingers entwine with mine. "I hate this guy. I can't stand him. Two minutes in a room with him, you'll see why. I only responded to his Facebook message to be polite, and then he just slammed me with message after message. My mom will give me shit if I don't respond to him, so I did."

"Your *mom* will give you shit?"

She looks away with a sigh. "Yeah. You'll see."

Jesus.

"Do I need to make it clear to this guy who I am?"

Do I need to make it clear to *her* who I am?

We've been dating now for a while, and we've moved

into an easy routine. I've asked her three times to move in with me, and she'll have none of it. She loves her friend Diana and is happy for her but insists the whole wedding and kid thing isn't her gig. I don't know how I feel about that. I only really know how I feel about her.

She leans in and puts her head on my shoulder. "Yes," she whispers. "*We* need to make it clear to *everyone.*" She sighs again. "Swear to God if this was anyone but Chantilly, I wouldn't be going."

"That bad?"

"That bad."

We drive in silence until the houses give way to nothing but a long stretch of road, lined with elegant trees that leave dappled shadows on the ground in front of us. To the right I see what looks like a barn, a stable with a white picket fence, though it doesn't appear there are any animals there. And further up, ahead, lays a creek, lined with rocks, and though it's far off from the main road, it looks like a wrought-iron bench sits alongside it.

"God, this is beautiful," I say.

"I know," she whispers. "That's my family home, up ahead."

And then I see the shadow of her house. Can I call it a house? A mansion is more like it. Estate? This is the biggest place I've ever laid eyes on. The balcony extends over the grass below, ivy hanging from the black fence that surrounds it. Huge glass windows dot the house, and to the left is a large, kidney-shaped pool. A garden flanks the right side, with a trellis laden with vines. Though it's early fall, roses still bloom at the entrance to the garden. Far, far in the back I see a small treehouse of sorts, a wooden structure beside a swing set that looks like a child's fantasy plaything.

I feel suddenly way, *way* out of my element. Why hasn't she told me this? Her family's fucking loaded.

"This is where you grew up?" I ask, incredulous, as we approach the locked gate.

"Well, one of the places where I grew up. We own a house in Maine, a vacation home in Florida, some property on the West Coast we traveled to, and um… a chalet in Paris." She says it all in a rush.

Holy *shit.* Wow.

"We went camping in the Berkshires of Western Mass," I say with a forced laugh. How could I have dated her for seven months, asked her to move *in* with me… fucked her more times than I could count… have actually thought about marrying her, and not known this about her? I've asked her about her family but she always evades questions. I knew they were wealthy and she didn't talk to them much and that she has no siblings.

That was it. We both worked so much I hadn't taken her to see my folks yet but planned to over the holidays.

"I can't believe I didn't know this about you," I say.

Her jaw tightens, and she looks back to me, pulling her hand away. "This is not something you didn't know *about me,*" she says. "And it's exactly why I *haven't* said anything to you. Because this isn't me. This is a small part of who I am, for the sole reason being that I grew up here. It doesn't define who I am even a *little,* and I've spent my entire adulthood distancing myself from this life that is no longer *me.*"

I'm not sure I agree. I clench my jaw. "Bea, I get that. And I respect it. Still, you grew up with bank, babe, and I should've known that."

She purses her lips and turns away. "Well now you know."

She's pushed it far enough. "Watch it, sweetheart." My

tone is hard, she knows better than to push me with the disrespect.

She sighs and nods. "I'm sorry, Zack." She takes my hand. "I'll behave."

"Good girl." I know this is not easy for her. I'll do the best I can.

We pull up to the gate. "Punch in..." she hesitates and releases a deep sigh. "Princess 0822."

That's her birthday.

"Princess?"

"Please don't ask," she whispers.

Something tells me pretty soon, I won't have to.

Chapter 5

Mom comes out to greet me the second Zack puts the car in park. She looks, as usual, completely stunning. Despite her age, her hair is still platinum blonde, and she's dressed like she just stepped out of a studio, in a form-fitting silver and moss-green dress that hugs her slim, svelte figure. Her skin looks as beautiful and unblemished as the last day I saw her, which, if memory serves, was over two years ago. I wonder if she got another injection of botox.

She looks, if possible, even haughtier than I remember, and a little thinner. Her blonde hair, once as golden as mine, looks lighter, whiter even. Her arms cross on her chest, and I can tell she's taking in Zack's coupe. I love driving in his car, and I like it so much more than the shiny Mercedes parked in the garage. I know the pristine leather interior still looks as if the car was driven off the lot. It's only one of several cars they own, but the Mercedes is the one they drive on "regular" days. It's the supermarket car. The Lexus or BMW accompanies them on travel; the limo escort when they go to a benefit or anything in the public sphere. They scorn little cars like Zack's and would be utterly horrified if they knew of my propensity for dirtying myself within the interior of a random Uber.

Zack whistles. "Holy shit. Is that a classic *Bugatti?*"

"Yeah," I say, bored. Whatever. So the car's worth more than most people's homes.

Zack's eyes widen. "For real?"

"Yeah." I couldn't care less about the car. The only memory I have of the thing was when I stole it my senior year in high school to escape with my boyfriend of the hour. They didn't care about the car and cared less that my boyfriend had dumped me unceremoniously when the homecoming queen flirted with him. They were appalled that I'd dated *someone below me*. I went to private schools, and the ex had gotten a full scholarship. He was a "charity student," according to my parents. I could still feel the pain of his rejection, the sting of my parents' scorn when I looked at that car.

Unpleasant memories settled on my shoulders at being in the presence of my parents' estate again.

"This was a mistake," I whisper to Zack. "I don't want to be here. We should've gotten a hotel and stayed just for the wedding. I should've skipped the rehearsal dinner and just gone to the wedding." The rehearsal dinner is here tonight, a catered party in the back planned for afterward. Chantilly had begged me to come, and I'd finally agreed.

"Come home, Beatrice," she'd begged.

"We can still leave," Zack says. He hasn't opened the door yet. "I'll make the plans right now. Wave to your parents, and we can—"

"Beatrice! How *are* you?" The high-pitched greeting of Aunt Veronica makes me nearly jump. "Get out of that car and let me see you!"

She's coming around the corner of the garage, a cigarette held in between her chubby fingers. Aunt Veronica is my dad's sister, a plump, fairly innocuous relative of mine who's every bit as rich as my father is. She's nicer, though. More real. And though she wouldn't know what to do in a taxi if her life depended on it, she was always good to me.

"Hi, Aunt V," I greet, shutting the door and bracing myself as she reaches me. She gives me a bone-crushing hug, then releases me and takes another pull on her smoke.

Zack shuts the driver's side door and comes around to us.

"Aunt Bea, meet my boyfriend, Zack."

Her eyes go wide, and her brows shoot up. "You brought a date, darling? Your mother didn't tell me."

"I kept it sorta quiet," I answer, as Zack extends his hand.

"Nice to meet you," he says. He's tired from all the driving we've done but still hot as hell with his sandy-brown hair falling over his forehead, his dark eyes, and the scruff that lines his jaw.

"*Very* nice to meet you," Aunt Veronica responds. She turns to me. "And honey? That was a good call." She turns around and we follow her after Zack gets our bags from the trunk. He hands me the tiniest one and takes the other four, and though I protest, he insists.

Mom stands at the top of the steps and waits for us. My stomach churns with nerves. Figures she can't be bothered coming down to see me.

"Who's here?" I ask Aunt Veronica.

"Oh, everyone," she says with a wave of her hand.

My stomach lurches. It isn't until we climb the stairs that lead to the balcony that we get a good glance at our backyard. She wasn't kidding. Literally *everyone* is here. My cousins, my aunts, my uncles, my grandparents. I'm suddenly eighteen years old again, and the years I've spent defining myself in NYC evaporate.

Zack raises a sandy brow at me but doesn't say anything.

"Hi, mom," I say, needing to get this over with. Zack puts our bags down and extends his hand.

"Mrs. Moore, nice to meet you."

She doesn't take his hand and merely points to the entryway door.

"You can tell your driver where to put your bags, Beatrice. You'll be staying in the guest room on the first floor."

I blink before I realize she's talking about *Zack*. She thinks he's my driver. Zack's brows shoot up, and he looks to me.

"Mom," I stammer. "This is Zack. He's my boyfriend, not my *driver*. God!"

She blinks, her lips thin, and her gaze narrows on him. I see his husky, seriously hot form in worn jeans and a faded rust-colored tee, and she, no doubt, sees nothing but *faded*. Zack stands his ground, holding his hand out, and still she doesn't take it. Anger coils in my belly and I fight the desire to slap her perfect face. I haven't even been here five minutes and she's already insulted Zack.

This was such a fucking mistake.

"Beatrice? Oh my God! Is that Bea?" A familiar, lyrical voice reaches my ears, and a blur of white and brown stun me before I nearly fall over in a tackle hug from my cousin.

I stand back and hold her at arm's length. "Chantilly? Oh my God. You look *amazing*, honey!" And she does. The last time I saw her she was a very curvy, wide-eyed high school senior, and she still looks the same, with her beautiful sky-blue eyes, thick, chestnut-colored hair that cascades down her shoulders, but she looks a little older, and she's lost a little weight. She wears a white lace sheath dress and silver flats. A corsage adorns her right wrist, the smell wafting up to me as she holds both of my hands in hers. "I'm *so* glad you came," she whispers, effectively turning her back on my mother, her eyes sincere and filled with joy. "I was afraid you wouldn't. It means so much to me."

I lean in and kiss her cheek. "Wouldn't miss it, sweetie. I can deal with them for a few days to see my baby cousin say *I do.*"

I pull back and reach for Zack, putting my hand on his arm. "Meet my boyfriend, Zack." Zack takes her hand in his and shakes and they exchange pleasantries as my mother bristles in the background. Zack looks hot as hell but sticks out in this crowd. I don't care. I *won't* care.

"Your boyfriend?" Chantilly asks. "Oh, it's so nice to meet you." She looks him straight in the eye. "And I'm glad you came with her." She leans in and whispers, "She shouldn't have to face them alone."

Before he has a chance to respond she releases his hand. "Oh, for goodness sakes, you guys haven't even put your bags away yet. C'mon, c'mon." She turns to mom. "They're staying in the downstairs guest room, right?"

Mom's lips are so thin I'm surprised she can still speak. "*She* is," she says, her back rigid. "I'll find another place for him."

"Mom, he stays with me," I begin, but she narrows her eyes.

"And somewhere along the line you married him without telling me?" she asks.

"Well, no, I—"

"Then he stays in another room." I feel as if someone's dumped ice water on me.

"Let it go, babe," Zack says in my ear.

Chantilly looks from me to Zack, and I make a decision. "Just put the bags in there for now, Zack," I say. "We won't be staying here. We'll stay at the hotel tonight."

"Good call," Zack says, but Chantilly's face falls.

"Oh, I'm so sorry, but all the hotels are booked from here and thirty miles out." Her face winces apologetically. "Big wedding." She sighs.

I swear I see my mother's lips curl up.

"Let it go," Zack says in my ear. "We'll survive."

He has no idea what he's getting into.

———

AFTER WE PUT our bags away, Veronica, my mother's housekeeper, finds a vacant room near mine for Zack to stay. We dress for the evening and freshen up, and he joins me in my room, shuts and locks the door.

"Charming family," he says, but his eyes are twinkling.

I groan. "You haven't met my dad yet. Maybe reserve your judgment until then." Apparently, dad was out with Uncle Herb the night before, and had more to drink than he had in years. Mom says he's "under the weather," and Chantilly confides with a laugh that both dad and Uncle Herb were "three sheets to the wind."

"You gonna be okay out there?" he asks, pulling me to his chest. I sigh into him.

"I don't know. I mean, God, Zack. I don't want to be here. I want to go home. I mean, back to *my* place. Anything but here. This is oppressive. And that was mom on her *best* behavior. She thought you were my driver! My *driver.*"

He shakes with laughter, holding me against him. "Eh, better for her to think I'm your driver than your dom."

I groan. "Oh my God. Don't even go there. Are you out of your mind?"

He shakes his head, tugs my hair back and his mouth meets mine. God, it feels so good to be kissed like this, right here, in my parents' house, as if doing this somehow tells them to fuck off and let me be. His tongue brushes mine, sending a shiver of arousal skittering down my spine.

"You're a good girl," he whispers, and as always when he says that, my throat tightens and warmth spreads through me.

I love you, I want to say, but I can't. Not now. It's too much. Too early.

"Thanks," I whisper back. "I'm *starving*. Let's go stuff our faces with canapés and then we can drown our troubles for a little while?"

"Sounds good." He leans in, his mouth to my ear. "Behave yourself, and I'll give you the very best stress relief a girl could ask for tonight."

I gasp. "You brought *things* with you?"

"This from the girl that brought her body weight in shoes and makeup? You expected your dom to go away with you and not pack some toys? Seriously?"

"In my *parents'* house?" The idea of me strapped spread-eagle to his bed makes my belly quiver.

He grins. "*Especially* in your parents' house."

He releases me, unlocks the door, and leads me back to the main entryway. "How will you be quiet?" I hiss in his ear.

His lips quirk up and he whispers back, "Doll, I'm not the one who'll have to be quiet."

My pulse spikes.

Is it bedtime yet?

"Is that my Trissy?"

Oh, *God*. He *didn't*.

"Hi, dad," I say with a forced grin. My father comes to me with arms outstretched, ignoring Zack and making a beeline to me. My dad is a large, balding man with glasses and ruddy cheeks, born of too much bourbon and Florida golfing. I left my childhood home and went off on my own because of the oppressive presence of my mother, her insistence on meeting her standards and expectations, and I still slam him in the same "judgy parents" camp, but damnit if my eyes don't water when I see my dad. I've missed him. I wonder why I've hidden from him for so long.

When he reaches me, he pulls me to his chest and kisses my forehead. I feel Zack beside me, watching this exchange and taking it all in. He didn't miss my mom's frost, and he isn't missing my dad's warmth.

"Dad," I whisper. "God, I've missed you." He smells so good, like I always remembered him. A mix of peppermint and bourbon and expensive cologne. I breathe him in, and for a split second, I'm a child again. I swallow hard against the lump in my throat. I should never have been away from him so long. He releases me and holds me at arm's length, peering down at me, his eyes filled with concern.

"Are you okay, honey? Are you well?" His voice is thick with emotion. "Happy?"

God, I'm a mess. He says one more thing and I'm gonna bawl in my daddy's arms like a little girl. "I'm good, dad," I whisper. "Real good. And I want you to meet someone."

I pull away from dad and reach for Zack. "This is Zachary Williams. He's a detective for the NYPD." I swallow. "My boyfriend." Zack takes my father's hand, and their eyes meet, both of them shaking firmly, and neither says anything at first. They're sizing each other up, and I'm holding my breath as they each make sure the other is someone who can be trusted. Zack breaks the silence.

"Pleased to meet you, sir," he says warmly.

My father smiles approvingly. "And you, Zachary. NYPD, eh?" He releases Zack's hand.

"Just Zack is fine, and yes."

"Leonard!" My mother's shrill voice makes all of us stiffen. My dad draws in a shuddering breath.

"Yes, dear," he says, closing his eyes briefly and pinching the bridge of his nose before turning to face her. My mother click-clacks her way over to us on her heels.

"We're out of ice. Have some of the help go get some," she barks out, then her gaze roams to me and Zack. She waves a dismissive hand. "Or maybe he'll do it."

My father's jaw clenches and Zack squeezes my hand. I open my mouth to protest, but my father speaks before I do.

"I'll go, and Zack will come with me."

My mother's lips thin and her eyes darken. "You can't leave our guests like that. I'm sure he can find ice without your help. It's a menial task, Leonard."

"Muriel, I'm sure he can, and I'm sure you'll do an excellent job entertaining in my brief absence." My father's voice holds a firmness I'm not familiar with, and I watch as my mother rolls her eyes and huffs out a breath, then marches away from us.

"I'll get my bag," I say, but my father swings his gaze to mine.

"No, just me and Zack, Beatrice. As much as I'd love to spend every second of your visit with you, you stay here and visit with your cousins."

I look up to Zack his warm eyes soften, and his lips quirk up. "See you in a few, Bea." He gives me a gentle kiss on the forehead, releases my hand, and follows my dad.

Before I know what's happening, they're talking about my dad's cars, and Zack's eyes light up like a little boy when my dad says they'll take the Bugatti. Ugh. *Showy*.

I stand, frozen, watching my father and Zack leave together. Something in my heart squeezes, and my fears only worsen. Was it a mistake bringing Zack home?

Chapter 6

Beatrice's father's a trip. He talks non-stop and shows off his Bugatti with a note of pride. He should be proud. It isn't every day someone drives a car that cost a cool mil. I insist he stays in the car while I grab the ice from the little market he drives to, and I'm not surprised there are people surrounding the car when I come out.

When we pull away, I feel a little like a celebrity. "Got her the year Beatrice was born," he says, as he pulls onto the main road. "Took good care of her, and now I could never part with her. She reminds me of my girl."

I've never ridden in a car like this. The leather-clad interior fills my lungs, the buttons on the dash gleaming chrome. He's taken good care of it. My hair whips in the wind as he's driving with the top down, despite the cool fall air. "Muriel won't ride in it. Says it messes with her hair and the smell of the diesel makes her nauseous."

"This is amazing," I say.

"Thank you," he says. His voice is reserved and coiffed, like fine wine, and I'm intimidated by the fact that this guy's filthy rich. What does he see in me when he looks at me? Does he think I'm good enough for his daughter?

"Her bringing you home is a big deal, you know," he says. "She and her mom don't get along."

"I gathered that."

"And she's never brought a guy home before."

Great.

"I didn't want her to make the trip alone," I explain.

Her father gives me a sidelong glance. "Good," he says. "I like that."

I may not have a million in my account in my favor, but I do care for his daughter. Hell, I adore her. I can't imagine letting anyone or anything hurt her, and that includes her Ice Queen of a mother. Leonard doesn't need to hear that part, though.

"Beatrice doesn't come home," Leonard says, as he pulls into his garage and parks the car. "I've tried to give her reason to. And let her know she's welcome anytime. But she doesn't do it." He shrugs. "She has her reasons. And I respect those reasons." He looks at me, and his jovial face sobers, eyes narrowed and jaw tight. "One thing you should know, Zachary." As a detective, I've studied these things before. I know how to read facial expressions. I know how to read body language. My instincts perk up. He leans in. "Keep her the hell away from Judson. You understand me?"

Immediately, I'm on alert. Beatrice and I will have a talk, and soon.

"Yes, sir," I say. "Anything I should know?"

Her father looks past me and sighs, deep in thought for a moment, before he responds. He shakes his head. "I don't want to overstep, or to make mountains out of molehills. But I don't trust the guy. You're a detective. And furthermore, you're a man." He shakes his head. "You'll see."

And he gets out of the car, just like that. He reaches for the large bags of ice, but I get them first, lifting both out easily. "I've got it," I say, and we head up to the deck. My stomach growls with hunger. I'm starving, and someone's grilling something that smells delicious. But first, I need to check on my girl.

I scan the deck for her after I drop the ice off by the coolers, and at first, I can't see her. There are so many people. Then I see the flash of a hand waving, and look to see Beatrice waving me down, all the way at the other end of the deck. She's in a crush of women dressed to the nines, and she's wearing some sorta ridiculous feathered mask up to her eyes, which she pulls away when she sees me heading in her direction. They're snapping pictures. A few guys dressed formally stand to the side, and I'm suddenly *way* underdressed here in the slacks and a polo shirt I changed into. I thought we were just meeting her family, maybe having dinner, and I wasn't planning on dressing up until tomorrow. But these guys are already dressed as if we were heading to see a show on Broadway.

One particular guy catches my attention. He's taller than the rest, and he's built. He could've been a quarterback or something. He's clean shaven and has a strong jaw, his eyes focused on the girls without humor. His suit is expensive, and even the way he holds himself is somehow above the rest.

Fuck me. My gut says this is him. I don't even need an introduction. The way he's staring at Beatrice, I know. It's Judson.

Beatrice lights up when she sees me. "Hey, Zack," she says, leaning in to kiss my cheek. I move my head as her lips come close and take her mouth with mine, and quickly wrap my hands around the back of her neck. I don't kiss her long, but anyone who's watching us—and I know at least one person is—knows this girl is *mine*.

She pulls away, breathless, and her eyes are bright with excitement. "Well *hello*," she says. "You missed me in the past fifteen minutes?"

"Course I did." I wrap an arm around her waist and take in the scene around me. Wait staff serve champagne in flutes, and plates decorated with white doilies of hors d'oeuvres. Elegant music plays below us, a five-string quartet set up on the sprawling green expanse of lawn. And this is just the rehearsal dinner? *Jesus.*

I see her mother watching us with narrowed eyes in one corner, but I ignore her. She's a bitch to Beatrice, so she can keep her narrow eyes and scorn. They don't touch me. It's the douchebag football-player guy approaching us now that has my full attention. His gaze intensifies, his jaw clenched. He's seen me kiss her, and he didn't miss a damn thing. I tighten my grip on her.

"God," she hisses out of the side of her mouth. "That's him." No shit.

I give him a full grin. *Come and get me, loser.* He seems momentarily taken aback by my smile, and halts for a split second, before he comes closer.

"Judson," Beatrice says, holding onto my arm as if I'm her lifeline. "How nice to see you." She's lying through her teeth, but I don't blame her.

The guy pushes past me, practically making me lose my balance, leans in and kisses Beatrice on the cheek. She gasps, and I barely contain the urge to yank him by his collar and break his nose. Something tells me that maybe wouldn't go over too well here. Beatrice, however, can hold her own. She shoves him away and steps back, her eyes flashing.

"Judson, this is Zack." She grits her teeth. "He's on the NYPD." It seems a random fact, but one she is proud to say. Good girl. I want this guy to fear me.

Fire flickers in the man's eyes for a split second before he extends a hand out to me. "Nice to meet you," he lies.

I take his hand and shake it firm enough for it to hurt. "Same to you," I lie back. The man's jaw clenches as he stares at me, and I swear there's something familiar in his eyes. Where do I know him from? Wherever it is, it isn't good, but my job's made me way too suspicious. Everywhere I go I see something or someone who sets me on edge. I don't like to ignore my instincts, but at the same time, I can't go chasing shadows. Could have something to do with the fact the guy just kissed and practically groped my girl.

"Beatrice and I go *way* back," he says, and there's something about the way he says it that dredges up a horrible vision of the two of them in bed together. I want to snap his fucking neck. "Did she tell you? She told me how excited she was to come see me this weekend."

"That isn't exactly—"

He talks over her. "And I looked forward to our reunion." He turns to her. "Bought a new Beamer, baby. You want to go for a ride?"

Baby?

Her jaw drops. If he thinks she's the kinda girl who's gonna get impressed with the car he drives, he really doesn't know her at all. He curls a lip at me, raking his eyes over my khakis and polo. "And who are you again? Jack?"

And for some reason, I lose my shit. I'm no longer the cool, calm, collected guy I was when we arrived. There's something wicked and enchanting about this place, and I wish to fuck I'd never come.

"Zack Williams," I say, meeting his gaze squarely. I step

toward him and I'm about to haul his ass down off this balcony and settle things like men, but Beatrice bristles beside me.

"Oh, just to say? One other thing I haven't told anyone yet," she says. "He's my *fiancé*."

She did *not*. I swing my gaze to hers, but she won't look at me. Her cheeks are flushed pink, her eyes wide and bright. She's trying to throw this guy off her game but shit, she just threw me off mine.

"Don't tell anyone," she says in a rushed whisper. "No one at all. It's still like a total secret."

Still a total secret? Fuck, it was a secret from *me*.

"Congratulations are in order, then," he says smoothly, and lifts his champagne flute. "To the happy engaged couple!"

A murmur goes up around us, and Beatrice makes a little squeak. She knows she's in trouble. I'm gonna spank her ass.

Chapter 7

Sometimes, I think I should seal my lips together with duct tape or something. No. Super glue. Maybe I was dropped on my head as a baby, because I say the stupidest things.

Fiancé. *Fiancé!* What the hell am I thinking? He hasn't even told me he loves me yet! I know he does. He takes such good care of me. He's so tender and strong and kind, and he's asked me to move in with him like twenty times.

And he's gonna spank my ass for what I just did.

"Always tell the truth, Beatrice," he says, in what I call the "old man" voice. The stern, almost paternal tone he takes with me sometimes when I'm being particularly childish and stupid. But it's one of the things I love best about him. He's so… *good.* So honest and kind, a man with integrity who has morals and structure and accountability.

My parents spoiled the shit out of me, and it wasn't until Carter left, and I chased him, that I realized how insulated my life was. Carter, the boy who was like a brother to me. The foster son my parents took in when my dad was running for Senate, to make themselves look good.

But money doesn't buy everything, and money didn't buy Carter happiness.

But I won't think about that now. I can't. My parents say he's "dead to them," and he hasn't returned my phone calls or texts or anything in so long, I wonder if he's okay. It was when he left and moved to NYC that I followed him. It was the first time I'd been in the inner city, and I knew after going there I needed to live there. I needed to be stripped of the princess bubble I'd been raised in. I needed to know how real people lived, how real people paid their bills. I needed to scrub my own floors and wash my own laundry and have to worry about things like budgets and rent payments. And I had. I'd scraped off my spoiled rich girl upbringing and made my way in the world.

But I fucked up. I forgot to pay my bills and didn't check my mail. I forgot to check my voicemail, and I'd killed four aloe vera plants in two months because I forgot to water them, and those bitches are hard to kill. I mean, they're desert plants. They're *meant* to thrive on hardly any water and still, I killed them.

And Zack... he's everything I'm not. He makes sure I take care of myself. He makes me set reminders on my calendar to do things. He checks to make sure I've done what I'm supposed to, that I don't overdraw my bank account or forget to go to my check-up at the doctor's. And I love him for it.

I look at him with an apology on my lips, and his eyes are gentle but stern. He knows I said what I did in desperation, but how are we going to get out of this now?

"You're engaged?" Chantilly's by my side and she's practically giddy, bouncing on her toes, her beautiful blue eyes alight. "Oh, Beatrice. And he's so hot, too!" A murmur goes through the crowd, but I can't look at anyone, can't talk to anyone. Zack's taking me by the hand

and pulling me to a secluded area below the deck, where a vacant bench sits among the waning garden, fall mums and greens blooming along the walk, their bright orange faces a herald of cold ahead.

My heart pounds as I walk with him. I know that look on his face means I'm in trouble, and the submissive in me cringes at facing him. I hate when I fuck up.

"Oh my God, I'm so sorry," I say. What's even worse is that I've gone ahead and made me his fake fiancée, which is presumptuous, even if it isn't real. We don't live with each other. We haven't declared our love for one another. And here I am, announcing in front of everyone that I'm *engaged?*

"Beatrice Ann," Zack groans, pulling out the middle name. God. I'm in worse trouble than I thought.

"Zack—"

"Uh uh. Listen to me." He pulls us to sitting on the stone bench, and a flood of memories blankets me. I remember sitting here the night Carter left, and we got a call from the police department that he'd been arrested. I remember my dad pacing that deck above, and my mother screaming at him from the doorway, telling him what an idiot he was for ever taking in a foster son to begin with. I remember sitting here the first day I started my period, on the cusp of womanhood. I couldn't talk to my mother about it, but I'd called Chantilly. She was younger than I was, but not so young she didn't understand what a big deal that was. She'd called Aunt Veronica, and we'd gone out for hot cocoa. She bought me a little pair of heart-shaped golden earrings I still kept in my jewelry box. And I remembered how she'd told me how proud she was seeing me grow to be a woman.

My mother never knew. She just must've magically assumed I'd grown up or something.

I sat on this bench doing Algebra homework. I'd had a tutor in high school for a while, since we were traveling to Paris for a time. I'd work out these problems, right here on this bench. It was my quiet spot. My mom hated coming down here because she said the soft soil around the bench soiled her shoes. I'd kick off my shoes and walk barefoot, reading reams of poetry written by Byron and Dickinson and Frost. I always fancied myself some sort of fairy down in the garden, a fairy whose wings hadn't yet grown.

Now here I am with Zack, my NYC Zack, who doesn't own a yacht or buy me diamonds but offers me something so much richer than anything I've ever owned.

And my Zack is angry.

"How could you say that, Beatrice?"

"I just blurted it out," I whisper, keeping my voice low. He speaks hardly above a whisper himself, not wanting to call attention to us. "I didn't mean it. I don't want you to think I expect—"

"It isn't about that, doll," he says dolefully, sitting down on the bench and pulling me to sit on his knee. Damnit, the gesture is so sweet, his pet name for me making me want to cry. I don't know how to respond, and I know there are people on the deck looking down at us, but I don't care. I want to sit with him like this. His arms go around my waist.

"You didn't tell me about any of this," he says, waving a hand around the back yard. "I mean, honey, your dad told me he owns a private *island.*"

"My *dad,* does," I say. "And he's only part owner."

His lip quirks up and I can see the stern expression he's wearing is threatening to break. He pushes his lips together and finally, bursts out laughing, his shoulders shaking from it. "*Part* owner of a private island. So glad you clarified that, babe. I feel *so* much better."

And suddenly I'm laughing and crying all at once. My head drops to his shoulder and he puts his arms around me. "I don't want to be here," I whisper. "It's great seeing Chantilly and dad, and everything, but this isn't who I am anymore, and it's painful to remember I ever was."

He hooks a finger under my chin. "Not gonna be the only thing that's painful, sweetie."

I pout a little and whisper in his ear. "Am I in trouble for all this?"

His grip tightens. "What do you think?"

I nod and snuggle deeper on his chest. I need this. I know I do. The accountability and rules and structure and *discipline.*

"I think I have never needed a good, hard session, more in my entire life," I say.

"I agree," he says grimly. "I'll take care of you, Beatrice. And you know what? We're not gonna clarify that we're not engaged."

I lift my head off his shoulder and stare at him. Is he saying what I'm thinking he is? But his eyes soften, and he shakes his head. "I'm not proposing. You know me better than that. I don't want to do it under duress. You know that, right?"

I nod, and my heartbeat quickens. "But while we're here, I guess it wouldn't hurt for them to think we're that committed to each other, especially if it gets Judson off your ass."

"Okay," I whisper. "Thank you."

"Alright, honey. Let's get this over with. And tonight, we'll talk."

I hop off his knee and take his hand, and high up on the deck, someone clangs crystal to get the attention of those around us. "A toast for the happy couple!" They say, and for a split second I wonder if they're talking about *us.*

But no. God, for a minute I completely forgot this was Chantilly's gig. They're the ones getting married tomorrow, not me, thank God.

I join everyone up on the deck and reach for my phone to take a picture of the happy couple, when a slew of notifications comes in all at once. What the hell? Frowning, I swipe at the phone. Notifications from Facebook, and emails, and a string of messages from Diana.

OMG. You got engaged? Baby. You DIDN'T TELL ME!

Ice skitters down my spine, a shiver of nerves. How did she know already?

I type quickly in response. *How did you know?*

I saw it on FB! Someone tagged you!

Dear God. I quickly look, and she's right and *holy shit* there's a picture of me sitting on Zack's knee on the bench, his head thrown back in laughter. That was like one minute ago!

It was… not true. It's a ruse. I said it to get an ex-boyfriend off my back!

She doesn't respond right away.

Um. Zack was okay with that?

I groan. *Um, no. What do you think?*

Sigh. Sorry, babe. Well, try to enjoy your visit as much as you can, and we'll sort this shit out later.

I love that she says *we'll* sort it out. This isn't even her problem to sort out, and yet she's helping me sort it out and hell, will it ever need sorting.

Thank you. <3

I take a deep breath, square my shoulders, and face my family.

⸻

"CLOTHES OFF," he whispers. It's late night, hours past the

time my parents and all the other guests have gone to sleep. I left my door unlocked and waited for Zack, and he finally came. He's wearing boxers and a t-shirt, standing with his hands on his hips, the door locked behind him now. No one will bother us. But with a house full of people, I have to be quiet.

I stand in front of my bed and take off my shorts and tank, whipping them behind me. He twirls a finger to the bed. "Present."

I shake a little, wondering if he'll spank me. I crave climbing over his lap and having him sort me out, but anything too loud and I'll die of embarrassment. I fall to the bed, chest down, ass up, and lay my arms out in front to present myself to him.

"I'm going to punish you, Beatrice," he whispers in my ear, his breath making my fine blonde hair skitter across my neck. "What I want to do is take you across my lap and give you a naughty girl spanking." My breasts swell and my stomach clenches. *Yess.* God, I want that so badly. "But it's better I wait until I get you home."

If he isn't going to spank me, what's he going to do, then? From the corner of my eye I see something dark in his hand, but I can't figure out what it is.

"Keep your head down," he orders. I listen, focusing on the sound of my breathing and my heartbeat. A soft, silky fabric moves across my cheek, then in my mouth, before he ties a knot behind my head as he gags me. He's used ball gags before, but this is softer. "You can't make noise, baby." Next comes the matching silk blindfold, and a scratching sound of metal. My belly quivers. Cuffs? But no. The next second, I feel cold metal on my chest and I gasp against the gag at the first feel of a nipple clamp. God! He's clamping me in *my parents' house?* He was smart to use the gag first or I'd have had something to say about this. But when the second clamp is in place, painful yet wildly erotic, I lose my ability to fight it. This hurts *so fucking good. So. Good.*

His palm cracks against my naked ass, one loud smack that anyone outside this room could hear, but after the deafening sound, I hear nothing outside my room. He pinches my ass now, then squeezes me, and it almost hurts as badly as a spanking. I moan against the gag, but the sound is so muffled, nothing escapes. "Need a good session with leather," he whispers. "But you'll have to take a rain check." He slips three fingers between my legs and chuckles. "That's my dirty girl. My little pain slut who gets turned on when I tell her I'll whip her ass."

I close my eyes, imagining he's standing behind me with his strap. It's wicked but hurts so good.

"Tomorrow at the wedding, you'll be on your best behavior," he says, pushing his fingers in me. My breath hitches and I hold onto the bedspread. "You'll drink no more than I allow and listen when I talk to you. You'll tell my anything I need to know, and if your mom gives you shit, you come to me." He's pumping into me and I can hardly listen to him. I want to tell him to stop talking about my mom when he's fingering me, but the damn gag prevents that from happening. So I just nod.

"Taking things to the next level, baby," he says. "You know that?" Do I? I don't respond. "I mean, after all, we're engaged now." He chuckles, his shoulders shaking, and he plunges his fingers so hard in me I buck on the bed. "Gonna fuck that pussy," he says, his voice a low growl. "Gonna make you come. And you'll take it without making a sound."

And that's exactly what he does, pushes down his boxers, holds me from behind, and plunges in deep. I can think of nothing else. My whole body is consumed with him, my mind filled with nothing but Zack. He works me over, hard and fast, and my need to come mounts. He shoves into me, and with two thrusts, I shatter. I moan against the gag, writhe under him as he comes hard and fast, yanking my head back with a tug on my hair that's nearly vicious as he spills inside me. He holds me against his chest, arms around me firm and secure. Too soon, he pulls out and with a quick flick of his fingers, unfastens the gag knotted behind my head.

"You get some rest, baby."

I turn over on my side. "I want you in my bed," I whisper.

He leans down and brushes my damp hair off my forehead. "Let's not push it, babe. Your mother already hates me, and your father might lose his mind."

"He can deal," I whine, but Zack shakes his head. "Get some sleep and I'll see you in the morning. Good night. *Fiancée.*" He grins and takes his leave, quickly exiting my room and going to his guest room. I stare at the back of the door and sigh. I don't like this at all. I don't want to be separated from him like this. And though he's laughing at the whole "fiancée" thing, something inside me lets lose a pang that makes me want to cry. I'll never be his fiancée for real. I don't want to get married. It just… isn't my thing.

This lie of mine will need to be remedied at some point, which will likely have to facilitate a fake break up or *something.* God. I'm such an idiot. My phone is buzzing and beeping, and I can't even deal. I silence it, roll over, then drift off into a dreamless sleep.

Chapter 8

Beatrice is off getting ready with the girls, and I'm sitting in the living room, or whatever the hell this room is. I'm not sure they have a living room in this place. That'd be too middle class. There's a study and an office, and a room with a huge grand piano, multiple bathrooms on every floor, and swirling, elaborate staircases that lead upward to other floors, which I haven't even visited. Mirrors hang on the walls, and crystal chandeliers in places. I even heard someone mention a pool downstairs. *Inside the house.* I've never been in a private residence like this before, and I'm a little stunned.

"Drink, Zack?" Beatrice's father has a tumbler with amber liquid and ice in a glass, which he sips from before he gestures to a doorway. "Come with me while we wait for the girls." I follow him, and he leads me past the ornate, carved book shelves and fireplaces to a small door in the corner of the room. "I'm taking you to what the girls call my man cave," he says with a husky chuckle. "Muriel won't grace my room with her presence, so it's sort of my escape.

You know. From when I need to get away from her. We all need one of those, eh?"

We don't all, but I could see why he would. He elbows me and gestures for me to go downstairs. Fortunately, he isn't waiting for a response, because I'm not sure what I'd say to him. Yeah, I've got friends I get together with and we do manly stuff, I guess. We shoot pool and drink beer and watch football games. But I've never wished I had a place to escape to as far as Beatrice is concerned.

I hear the sound of murmured voices as he takes me downstairs. "Beatrice used to love to hide out down here," he says in the darkened stairwell. His voice is strangely thick with emotion. "She said she liked a place that was away from her mother, too." He pauses as we near the end of our trek downstairs. "Muriel means well but can be a little overbearing."

A little?

We've arrived. No less than half a dozen guys in suits sit at the bar, and I recognize the man pouring drinks behind the counter as Chantilly's father. Seems everyone's making themselves at home. I walk toward the bar when I recognize Judson, but I've learned to mask emotions, to not show when things take me off guard. I don't like this asshole at all.

"Hey," he greets. "Sounds like we'll be celebrating another family wedding soon, eh? What's your drink?"

I gulp. Jesus this is gonna be hard to untangle. "Just a beer," I say with a smile. "Thanks." I won't answer the question about the engagement.

The other men lift glasses and we toast, then I take a good pull on my drink. Jesus, this is good stuff.

"When are your plans?" Judson asks, sitting on a stool beside me.

"We haven't set a date yet," I say, which is completely

the truth. Hard to set a date when you're actually not even engaged. Judson's eyes are on me, narrowed, and he plays it cool.

"Yeah, let's toast the happy couple," he says. There's something sinister at play here, but I have no idea what.

But before we can say anything else, a door opens, and I catch a glimpse of the cars in the garage, before I realize it's Beatrice who's racing in. Her beautiful blonde hair is tucked up in this intricate woven pattern, little curls framing her face, tiny white roses studded throughout her hair. Her cheek are flushed, her eyes bright. She's wearing a dusky pink, fitted sheath dress that enhances her blonde hair and pink cheeks, and I want to pick her up and sit her on my knee, then wrap my arms around her so no one else looks at her.

She comes straight to me.

"Hi, guys," she says to the room around us. "I just need to talk to Zack for a minute. Everyone good?"

Murmurs and nods go up around us, and then she comes to me. "I can't find my purse," she whispers in my ear. "I swear to God I had it in my room and now it's gone."

I sigh. Not a week goes by where she's not losing something—her keys, her phone, her bag. I'm used to it. I give her a nod with the patience I've learned from dealing with this so many times. "And the last place you remember having it?"

"My room. I know it," she says. "I put my makeup on and checked my cell," she says, drawing closer to me and whispering in my ear. "This engagement thing has gone *viral*. Someone made a YouTube video of us, with pictures of us here, and music, and a whole bunch of people commented *congratulations*. Zack, we have a *Facebook page.*"

What?

I stifle a groan. Ok, so maybe this has gotten out of hand. "I'd show you," she mutters. "But my bag is *gone.*"

"Ok, it isn't gone. We'll find it."

"But Zack!" She whispers. "The girls are getting into the limo *now.*"

"All good, babe. I'll stay here and find it and meet you at the wedding."

She looks up at me. "Really?"

"Of course. It's an important thing you need. I don't mind."

"I'll help you look." We both look over, and Judson is standing nearby, watching us. His lips are tight, his eyes curious, but he seems friendly enough.

"Let him, son. Not much time," her father says.

Yeah, I totally don't want to do that but it's likely the smart thing to do and I like her father.

"Ok, thanks."

He nods. "I'll help you." Well, if this isn't a chain of events. But I'm foolish to say no.

"Yeah, man, thanks."

Everyone else finishes their drinks and heads out. Beatrice leans in, gives me a kiss on my cheek, and I want to do more than kiss her cheek. She smells like lilies and lemons, clean and fresh and intoxicating. "You behave yourself while you wait for me," I whisper in her ear. "And we're gonna have a talk later about you taking care of your things." I'm not really upset with her, but know she needs a reminder of who's in charge before she goes. It keeps her steady and calm. She casts her gaze down and whispers in my ear. "Yes, sir. Thank you." She needed to say it. I give her an appreciative kiss on her cheek. "Ok so it's a small, quilted silver clutch," she says, and she leaves.

What the fuck is quilted silver? I can go by silver though.

Her father and uncle and everyone else follow, but Judson still sits on the stool, and now he's staring at me.

"You got time for another drink?" Judson asks.

I shake my head. "Not really. Gotta find her bag and get to the wedding. Let me see if I can find it upstairs, and then we'll head out?"

I hope I can find it. "Yeah," he says, eyes narrowed on me. I've finely honed my skills, so I know when someone's lying, and this guy's extended friendship is so thin it's nearly transparent.

"You joining me?" I ask. He shrugs, pushes his glass on the counter, and follows me.

"She always was sorta flighty," he says.

I feel myself bristle. I'll give him flighty, right to his high-and-mighty jaw. "She isn't flighty," I snap. "She sometimes forgets things because she's got a million things on her mind." My voice is sharper than I intend.

"Right," Judson says, in a voice laced with judgment. I leave the bar and bump into the wall, setting a photo off kilter. I turn to straighten it and freeze. It's a picture of Beatrice with another man. He's young, and attractive, and the two of them are with her parents at some sort of beach home. Who is this? I've looked at lots of pictures of Beatrice upstairs, but this is a new one. And it's down here, hidden in the man cave, where Muriel can't see it.

I don't like the way she looks standing beside another man. The guy has a shock of jet black hair and is tall and lean with a swimmer's body. He's leaning in and kissing her cheek, and something in me flares to life. I want to shove this nameless person away from Beatrice and show him she's mine. I suddenly hate that I've let her go to the wedding alone and wish I hadn't offered to stay behind. But the truth is, the sooner we leave this place filled with demons and ghosts of Beatrice's past, the better.

"Her room?" Judson asks.

I nod. "So she says. I'll go to her room and look, and you go to the main living area and look."

"You got it, chief," Judson responded, his voice laced with sarcasm. I clench my jaw and ignore him. We just need to find her bag and get out of here. I go through everything in her room, even her shoe bag and clothing bag, but see nothing. I rifle through the closet and with chagrin realize there's a whole pile of pictures in here, too, with the Superman-lookalike guy in several of them. What the fuck?

Her bag is nowhere to be found. I run a hand through my hair, exasperated, when I hear Judson calling from the other room. "Found it!"

He comes in with the silver bag in hand. "She left it out on the porch. Must've been taking pictures or something," he says. I don't trust him, though. How convenient that she lost her bag and he was the one who randomly found it?

"Thanks, man," I say, reaching for it. He hands it to me, and I unzip it. There are her keys and phone and makeup and cell. Something's wrong, though. I take out her cell and eye it carefully, not turning it on. The case is askew, like someone's torn it off, and then put it back on in a rush.

Sometimes I hate my job. For all I know, this is just in my head, seeing ghosts where no one else does, guessing everyone's motives and intentions. I sigh. I wish I could take things at face value, but I can't. It's just who I am, how I'm wired. Next, I open her wallet while Judson stands, his arms crossed on his chest.

"You think I went through it?" He asks, he is voice tight and angry.

"Didn't say that," I say. "But I'm just making sure no

one did." I open her wallet, and everything's there. I made her hit the ATM the day before and I knew she got out one hundred dollars in cash for the trip and clearly, she hasn't spent it. Every bill is still there. Somewhat satisfied, I put it back in her bag.

"Ready to go?" Judson asks, his lips pursed. He's turned away from me. Yeah, I'm ready. Her phone buzzes and I look at the screen. Jesus. She has thirty-nine notifications. This is out of control.

"Bag looks good with your outfit, officer," Judson says with a huff of laughter.

"Thanks," I say without responding to his assholery. This guy is not my friend. I'm not even going to pretend otherwise.

When we arrive at the wedding, I ask her to look through to make sure everything's there.

"Seeing ghosts again, honey?" she asks, her blue eyes bright.

"Yeah, babe. It's my job. Making sure the ghosts aren't giving you shit."

She looks through her bag. "I think it looks normal. Can't say I would notice if someone stole a mint or something."

I smile at her. "Good."

I take my seat behind the others, after giving her a parting kiss on the cheek. She's the most beautiful one of the bunch, and my heart swells to see her standing, looking at her cousin with damp eyes and pink cheeks, like a little girl about to ride the carousel. She doesn't want to be married, she's said, but I can't help but wonder what it would be like to be the one standing up there with her, taking her hands in mine and pledging lifelong devotion, then sliding the band around her finger.

I swallow hard, the rest of the details a blur, then before I know it, a groomsman is holding up the hands of the bride and groom and cheers erupt around us. Beatrice finally joins me.

"God, I need to find a seat," she mutters. "My feet are killing me, I'm dying of starvation, and my mouth is so dry I feel like someone's stuffed it with cotton."

"Cheers for the happy couple!" God, they're starting again? And no, this time they're not talking about the bride and groom, but someone at our table has a flute of champagne they're raising in our direction. I see Beatrice's mom narrow her eyes at us from another table, her lips so thin it's almost comical. I groan, take my flute, and play along.

I eye everyone in the room as I take a sip of my champagne, and now that Beatrice is done with pictures, I hold her elbow. I don't give a shit if everyone's going to think we're engaged. Hell, I want them to know she's with me. I don't trust these people. And she isn't herself around them. She's skittish and on edge, and I need to get my girl alone again to get her back on track.

"Relax," I whisper in her ear. "We'll be out of here soon."

"It just sucks," she whispers back. "I wanted this to be nice. I wanted to be happy for Chantilly and give her my support. But everyone's talking about yachts and vacation homes in Europe and the size of their diamonds."

"You know what they say about size," I quip.

She smiles and giggles, then takes another sip of champagne.

"God, you're gorgeous," I remind her. The dress she's wearing looks like it was a custom fit, a low scoop-neck in the front that shows the barest hint of cleavage accented with a long silver necklace. She has dangly earrings that sparkle when she turns her head, and a little pair of matching silver heels. I place my hand on her lower back and draw her closer to me.

Mine.

"Yes," comes a haughty voice behind us. "So I've heard." I look to the side and see her mother eyeing us. A tall woman with silver hair piled on her head turns and looks at me and Beatrice, purses her lips, then heads our way. She's heard what?

"Oh, God," Beatrice whispers to me. "Just don't talk to her. She's like a Siren or something and will lure you in then dash you on the shore."

And she grew up around these people?

"Zachary," the woman says, holding out her hand. "I'm Muriel's best friend, Marjorie. I'm told you've proposed to Beatrice?" Her hand is ice cold when I take it in mine, her eyes piercing me.

"Fairly recently," I say, giving her a courteous shake of the hand before I turn away from her. "We haven't set a date yet."

"And no ring either, I see?" She looks down her nose at Beatrice, whose cheeks are flaming red. She's got a shit poker face.

"My mother always said there was no engagement without a ring and a date. Otherwise, it's just child's play."

I'll give her fucking child's play.

"There were a lot of things your mother said," Beatrice says with a fake smile plastered on her face. "One of them was, if you don't have anything nice to say, don't say anything at all." She tosses her head and turns her back to the woman.

"Beatrice," her mother hisses, her eyes narrowed on us. She's unable to hide the outrage written on her features. I won't rescue Beatrice this time, or make her behave, either. I'm proud of her.

"Want to get another drink, sweetheart?" I ask her. She nods eagerly, and I turn my full body to her, aware of the women staring at us. I wrap a hand around the back of Beatrice's neck, pull her to me, and kiss her on the lips, hard and possessive. I hear them both gasp, but when I pull away, Beatrice's eyes are aglow, her cheeks flushed. It was worth it. Without another glance back at the women, I take Beatrice by the hand, and lead her to the bar. Her father lifts a hand in greeting. He may be a fool to be married to the Ice Queen, but I think he's good people.

I wave back, and when we hit the bar, order her a glass of wine. We'll drink and be merry and dance, then get the fuck out of here.

"You hungry?" I ask her.

"No. I've lost my appetite somewhere around stock market and diamond carats," she says. "And they're serving prime rib which is like the grossest thing ever." I snort. I can handle prime rib, but I'm as ready as she is to get out of here.

"How about we wish the bride and groom well," I say, "then we get our bags and just leave?"

Her eyes light up, and she grins at me, her voice low and seductive. "Zack, that's the sexiest thing I've ever heard you say."

I grin at her. "I'm offended," I whisper in her ear. "I've definitely got better moves than that."

She goes up on her tiptoes and kisses my cheek. I want to pull her closer, hold her against me, and never let her go.

"Hey," she whispers in my ear. "I know of this burger joint nearby. They have the best fries on the planet."

"Let's go."

We gather our things and she quickly hastens to her father. "We need to go," she says, and the relief written on her features makes me want to wrap her up in my arms, poor thing.

"Going? So soon?" Beatrice stiffens next to me. We turn to face her mother, who eyes us both coldly, her eyes narrowed. "Zachary, it isn't fair of you to take my darling daughter away so soon."

"Mother, he isn't taking me away. I have work to do in the morning, and we need to go." Beatrice's voice is icy in return.

Her mother's eyes become nothing but slits. "Since when was your job more important that your family?" She laughs mirthlessly. "Oh that's *right*." The laughter ceases and her voice sharpens. "*Always.*"

Me? I've had enough of this shit.

I reach for her mother's hand and shake it firmly, though she tries to pull away. "Pleased to have met you, Mrs. Moore". She tries to pull away, but I don't let her. "Your daughter's a grown woman now, Mrs. Moore. And I'm *really* goddamned proud of her. She's worked her ass off to get to where she is, dropped everything to come see her cousin get married, and now I'm taking her home." I hold her hand a bit longer than necessary, making sure she meets my eyes. I finally release her hand and her mother huffs something out, opens her mouth to speak, but I spin Beatrice around so both of our backs are to her now.

We say good-bye to her dad, and she wishes Chantilly well. Fortunately, Chantilly is surrounded by people, and has lots to do, so though she says she's sad to see Beatrice go, it's not too hard for Beatrice to take her leave. I can feel Beatrice's excitement just holding her hand. Poor thing. She's dying to rid herself of this, the memory of her past, the judgment from people she no longer shares anything with other than in name.

Chantilly kisses her cheek and gives me a big hug. "Be good to her," she says. "And I want the scoop on the wedding plans. Got it, honey?" she says to Beatrice. Beatrice promises she will.

I take her by the hand, and we go to leave. I feel someone's eyes on me, and quickly scan the room. Judson stands at the bar, glass to his lips, eyes unwaveringly on us. I look back at him and try to stare him down, but his gaze doesn't waver. Pissed off, I wave my hand at him. He simply sips his drink. Asshole.

The second we leave the hall; Beatrice's step is lighter, and she exhales. My heart goes out to her. She needs a good, hard session to calm her, but what she needs most of all is to be removed from this toxic environment.

"Oh *shit*," she says, screeching to a halt. She looks up at me sheepishly.

What has she done now?

"Your bag?" I ask with a sigh. She nods.

"Beatrice," I say warningly. My patience is wearing thin. "Where'd you last have it?"

"Welllll," she begins, and shoves her finger in her mouth, chewing on her nail. "Um…" her voice drops. "I don't know."

I sigh. "This is getting kinda old, you know."

"I know, I know," she says, and her eyes water. Damnit. The only time I like to see her cry is when she's tied up and scening, and only then because she needs the release. This tugs at my heart strings.

"Just so much… stress," she whispers.

"I know, baby," I say, taking her by the hand. "Now come on, let's go back and find your bag." But it doesn't take long at all. There's a pile of bridesmaid's shrugs and bags and stuff in the room where they took the pictures.

"You girls are just begging for someone to come in and swipe this stuff," I say with a sigh. "Seriously?"

She looks at me apologetically, and I swear with the light behind her making her blonde hair almost white, her blue eyes shining like moonbeams, she looks like a fairy. I reach out and tuck a stray strand of hair behind her ear. "It's all good, babe. Find your bag, and let's get the hell out of here."

She picks it up, leans over to me and kisses my cheek. "You're a good man, Officer Williams." She pulls back and takes my hand and we head to the car again. "This is weird," she says, and she pulls out a large green envelope. "Someone put something in my bag?"

"You sure it's for you?" I ask. My senses are on high alert. I don't like this.

"My name's on it," she murmurs, standing still as she slides her finger under the flap. "And… yours is, too. Says *Zack and Beatrice.*"

I give her a nod. "Go on. Read it." She rips the flap and pulls out a large black card with silver lettering that reads *Congratulations.* I raise a brow at her. The script below is cryptic.

"Congratulations to both of you. You deserve each other."

What the hell is that?

"Well. That's… nice?" she says, shoving it back in her bag.

"Not signed?"

She shakes her head. "Not signed." So weird.

"Give it to me," I say.

"Zack, what are you gonna run a print scan on it or something? See who left it?" That's not a bad idea. "Don't you think that's like way overkill? Just a card from someone who cares about me. Could've been anyone. They must've just wanted it to be anonymous is all."

Her bag's gone missing twice and the second time, someone left an anonymous card with a cryptic message? Not overkill at all. I want to get her home, and I wanna do it now.

Chapter 9

"Yes, of course, Mrs. Beauregard. I'm happy to thin your hair a bit." I speak so loudly I'm practically screaming, as Mrs. Beauregard is nearly deaf. I still work as a hairdresser a few days a week, though I'm transitioning to full-time work at the gym now.

"What?" Mrs. Beauregard croaks. She's ninety years old if she isn't a day, and as many pounds soaking wet, and the sweetest client I have. She comes every Monday morning like clockwork for her hair appointment, and every few weeks she gets a haircut as well. I move to pick up my scissors, feeling the burn across my back and ass as I do. Zack worked me over good the night before with the flogger until I was a puddle of goo in his hands, boneless and in a state of utter bliss. It was hard waking up this morning to him gone, but he had to catch up on the work he missed over the weekend, so he was up and out early. No one can see the marks he left on me, but I can feel them, the stripes from the lash and bite marks he left all over my belly and waist. I smile softly to myself.

"Hand me my bag, please," Mrs. Beauregard asks. I

reach for her bag and hand it to her, a momentary flash of panic causing me to draw in breath. Where's *my* bag? Honest to God if I misplace it one more time, Zack's gonna give me a real spanking, not the kind he gave me last night but punishment. I give Mrs. Beauregard her bag, then quickly scan the place for mine. I find it, tucked under the desk where I normally keep it. Honest to God, some days... I'm glad Zack isn't here to see.

My phone buzzes. I'm expecting Zack to call. "Hey," I say, without looking at the Caller ID. But no one says anything. So weird. I look down at the phone and see that the number is blocked. Huh. I put my bag right where I can see it and shove my phone in my pocket, then focus on finishing up my clients. It's an early night tonight. I'm heading out to do a dress-fitting with Diana, and I need to try on my bridesmaid dress, so I'm taking off early.

"Good night, Chloe," I say, waving to the young, twenty-something brunette who waves back at me enthusiastically. She's taking over while I go meet Diana. I exit the main door, and take a left, heading to where I know I parked the car. I rarely drive to work but needed to be able to get to Diana's in time, so Zack let me borrow his. I stare. His car is gone. Frowning, I look stupidly behind me as if somehow the car has come to life and is hiding behind me or something.

"What the fuck?" I wonder, looking around the parking lot again. I *know* I parked it here. I walk from one row of cars to the next, looking for his car. I know I parked it here, because I remember grabbing the last space under the "two hour parking only" sign. What the hell am I going to say to him? *Hey, sorry, but I actually lost your car?* Like *that'd* go over well.

And then I see it. Easily halfway across the lot, parked rather haphazardly, is Zack's car. I must be going out of my mind. I had to have driven it there. I mean, who forgets where they parked a car? Ok so actually, *me*. I haven't driven much lately, since NYC is so congested and difficult to drive in, and I'm out of the routine, but *still*. Against my better judgment, though something warns me not to, I walk to the car. I look to makes sure no one's in it, and when I arrive, my heart hammers in my chest. I'm going crazy. This is stress, and just a figment of my imagination. There's no way someone got my keys, *drove his car*, and then parked it somewhere else. But when I arrive, I see a familiar green rectangle on the passenger seat. It's another envelope.

With shaking hands, I open the door, pick up the card, and read it.

You really should be more careful, princess. My hair stands on end. Who *is* this? Who's doing this to me? My hand shaking, I dial Zack. It rings and rings, as I look frantically about me. God. *I need him to answer.*

"Hey, babe."

"Zack," I say in a whisper, so relieved the breath leaves me at once. I keep looking around the parking lot. "Someone moved your car."

I can *hear* him freeze on the other end of the line, the energy between us crackling. "What are you talking about?"

I fill him in quickly, my voice shaking.

His voice is a razor's edge. "Where are you now?"

"At work," I whisper. "I didn't park here. I know I didn't."

"*Are you in the car?*" He's moving now. I can hear him say something to someone else and hear the sound of a door slamming.

"Yes."

"Lock your doors and you do not move until I come

and get you."

"Yes, sir," I whisper, not even knowing what I'm saying. I slip automatically into submissive protocol hearing his command. Fear prickles down the back of my neck. I hear a scratching sound behind me and I whip my head around, convinced someone's in the car, my breath caught in my throat. But no, I'm alone. No one's here but me. Someone on a bike rides behind me. For God's sake, it's daylight out and I'm losing my mind.

"I'm coming to you immediately. I've got a friend on the corner, sending him to you before I get there." His voice gentles. "Baby?"

"Yes?" I whisper, a lone tear rolling down my cheek. I hate this.

"You're gonna be okay. I've got you. You hear me?"

"Yes. Okay. Yes, sir."

"Stay strong, baby. Do not get out of the car until I get there."

"I will," I whisper. I'm so cold. Nausea rolls in my stomach. A siren sounds nearby, and flashing lights come into the parking lot so quickly, I wonder how they got there. I'm in a sort of daze, waiting for Zack. Even though I *see* the flashing lights and *hear* the sound of sirens, I still jump and stifle a scream when someone bangs on my window. A uniformed officer waits on the other side. Zack's friend.

I go to unlock my door but then freeze. He said not to leave the car until he came, not his friend. I roll the window down a crack.

"Yes?"

"Ms. Moore?"

"Yes."

"Officer Williams sent me to you. Are you okay?"

I nod my head. "I am. But he told me not to get out of

the car until he came himself."

The officer nods. "There's no need for you to get out of the car yet. Stay here while we investigate the surroundings." The lights on his cruiser are flashing, and it sets me on edge. It's congested and busy here in the city, and people are starting to take notice. I pick up my phone and call Chloe in the salon. I can see her from the doorway.

"Chloe?"

"Babe, what's going on?" I can hear her snapping her gum and envision her standing with her hands on her hips.

"Someone moved my car on me. It wasn't where I parked it before."

"You sure you didn't just forget?"

"Positive. Whoever did it also left a card on the seat for me."

"Son of a bitch. I'll beat them senseless, they lay a hand on you."

I just nod mutely. I want Zack.

"You call your man?" She knows he's an officer.

"He's on his way, and he's the one that sent the officers here. They're investigating now."

"Okay, honey. He's a good one. Listen to him and take care of yourself, okay?"

"I will," I whisper, and I hang up the phone.

I open my bag to take out a piece of gum, something to chew so I can calm my nerves, and nearly drop my bag. Cinnamon gum is in place of my usual peppermint.

I hate cinnamon. I never buy it.

Someone's fucking with me, and it scares the shit out of me. I stifle a sob, shove it back in my bag, and slam my bag on my seat. It's then that I see him unfolding from a cruiser, his dusty brown hair askew, eyes zoned in on where I sit. The other men look to him and they have a quick conversation. He sweeps his hand across the parking lot and the other officers practically salute him, jumping to do what he says. I want him for myself. I want him to come to *me*.

He makes his way over to the car, and still, I don't move until he taps on the window. I unlock it and step out of the car. He reaches for me and pulls me close. "Baby. You ok?"

"Yes," I saw with a shuddering breath. "They were in my bag, too. Someone's touched my things." He listens while I explain about the gum.

"And no money or credit cards gone?" I check quickly and shake my head.

"No."

"Then this is someone who's out to fuck with you, not someone looking to rob you." He swears under his breath. "You're coming home with me tonight, sweetheart. I'll have someone go to your place tomorrow, and get what you need, okay?"

I nod, so relieved he's here but so freaked out by what's going on.

He has me get in a cruiser, takes the keys, and instructs his men dust his car for prints. I kinda think it's a big undertaking for something seemingly small, but he can do it, so he does. We drive to his place and he's quiet, his jaw tight, for most of the drive. "You saw nothing out of place?"

"No. I wish I had. I just get zoned in on what I'm doing."

"It's normal. You had no idea anything would be off. All good." I feel so much calmer with him here. "They left you a note on your seat? Then it's someone who knows you or at least follows you on social media or something." He's piecing things together, but not drawing any conclusions.

"Yeah."

"Yes. Have you talked to your mom or dad?"

"No, but why would that change anything?"

He doesn't respond at first. "Just wondering."

"Zack, are you implying that they are somehow involved in this? C'mon."

His tone is curt when he interrupts me. "I'm not implying anything. I'm asking all the questions, because that's my job." He gives me a sidelong glance. "And it's also my job to help you."

I'm immediately chastened. "Okay, yeah. I get it. Someone called me, too, but the caller ID didn't show a name, and they didn't say anything."

He growls low.

"I need to call Diana," I whisper. "I'm supposed to have a dress fitting tonight."

"Not tonight you don't."

"Zack..."

"Beatrice, do not push me right now. I'm pissed this happened, I want the fucker who's screwing around with you behind bars, and I'm not gonna let you outta my sight until that happens."

Just. *Great.*

"Then come with me to the dress shop. I mean... you *are* the best man. And you don't want me going back to the goth line, do you?"

He huffs out a breath. "Fine."

I try to lighten the situation. "Not sure it's your cup of tea, honey, but you might find the shop is exactly what you needed. You know, try on a few tuxes or something? Feel like a million bucks?'"

He snorts. "Yeah, right."

He gets a call and takes it, as I punch in the dress shop address on the GPS and as the phone lights up with a map, he begins to drive. "No one suspicious came your way?"

"Not that I noticed, no." We're in NYC. There are people from every eclectic walk of life here, and I have long since stopped paying attention to anyone suspicious. Maybe a bad habit.

"Any other strange phone calls?"

"Nope." I look out the window. It unsettles me that this happened after I went to my parents' house. Surely no one I knew would be stalking me like this? Even Judson in all his jerk face glory wouldn't pull this shit.

We circle the building until we find metered parking, neither of us speaking. Zack parks the car, opens the door for me and I exit, when my phone rings. I look at the ringer and don't recognize the number. Zack freezes, eyes on me.

"You know the caller?"

I shake my head.

He clenches his jaw. "Let it go to voicemail."

I do as he says and watch as the voicemail notification comes up on my phone.

"Now check it." I love that he protects me, but I don't like being with this terse, angry Zack.

I put the phone up to my ear. I don't know what I expected, but it sure as hell wasn't the voice I heard next.

"Bea. It's me. Carter. Called because the rumor mill says you're engaged. I just wanted to say congratulations. I'm back in the city. Maybe we can meet up sometime? I'll call you again."

I nearly drop the phone. I haven't heard from him in so long. Carter, my foster brother, the boy I grew up with when I was a teen, who jumped so far off the rails when he was in high school, he stole everything he could from my parents and took off. We didn't hear from him for years, and my parents don't acknowledge they ever had anything to do with him. But he was like a brother to me.

I hang up my phone in a daze and stare at it.

"Who was that?" Zack asks.

For some reason, I don't want to tell him. Not here, not now, when we have only minutes to talk privately and I can't really tell him much of anything. I don't want to talk about it, so I shrug. "Just an old friend." He gives me a probing look but then his phone rings and catches his attention.

The doors to the elevator open, and I follow Zack into the hallway, shaken. I don't want to tell him it was Carter on the phone, as he'll ask questions and I'm not up for discussing anything right now. Instead, I look around me at the interior. This place is gorgeous, and I could take in every detail for days. Plush, carpeted floors, in deep hues of burgundy and gold, vibrant wall art, light strings of instrumental classical music playing in the background. The door to the glass elevator closes, and I look at the buttons that shine like diamonds in the light.

His phone is up to his ear. "Thanks, man. Yeah. Okay, later." He looks quickly to me, his voice still tight. "Got the prints, now sending to see if we can identify anyone."

"How long does that take?"

"Two to three days."

"*What?*"

He raises a brow as the elevator swoops upward. "Standard procedure, babe. Just the way things go. Now be a good girl, try on your dress, do whatever dress shit you need to do, and we're out of here."

I know it isn't his fault, but I'm pissed at pretty much everything. I huff out a breath. "*Fine.*"

I push past him as the doors to the elevator open, but as I march away I feel strong fingers grasp my wrist. The hall is lined with doorways. He pulls me into an empty one. "Beatrice, *enough.*"

I try to pull my wrist away, but his grip is too firm.

I'm angry at everyone, and everything. Whoever moved the damn car and scared me shitless, my brother for deciding he'd call me out of nowhere, Zack for not calling my bluff on the engagement, and that doesn't even make sense to be mad at him. It isn't his job to handle my shit. Still, I think I worry a little that it's because he doesn't want it to be a fake. We've been "sorta dating" for months now, and he wants more, but do I? He's been hounding me to take our relationship up a step, to move beyond the casual thing we have, and I've resisted so hard. Why?

"Just let me go, Zack." My voice is tight and wavering, and I'm not sure if I mean for him to let go of my wrist or *let me go.* Leave me alone. Let me fend for myself.

I don't know what I want anymore.

"No. You calm the hell down and listen to me." I look into his eyes, and some of my anger melts a little. The man has dominated me so many times I don't remember, spanked my ass and tied me up and had his way with me. Hell, I respond without thought to his fingers snapping. So when he gets bossy on me, my body responds without my consent. The anger in me quiets because I know what happens if I push him. He's my dom. He doesn't care where we are. If I don't behave, he'll find a way to make sure I do.

And fuck if I don't need exactly that.

Exactly that.

I stare at him, my chin quivering. Leaning in, he takes my chin between his thumb and forefinger and I can't look away. His voice rumbles over me, commanding every part of me to attention. "We're here because you promised your friend you'd show. I'm with you, and Tobias is here. Between the two of us, you're safe right now. I'm not here because I want to be." He inhales, his broad shoulders straightening, then lets out a quivering breath, his anger tightly controlled. "If I had my way, you'd be locked up where no one could even fucking breathe the same air you do."

My heartbeat quickens.

He continues. "The last thing I need from *you* now, little girl, is a bratty attitude. You give me shit, and you're getting your ass spanked. Am I clear?"

Little girl from him is rare. He's like seven years older than I am, but still, when he says it, it makes me feel little. Chastened. And I know I'm being a bitch.

I swallow, try to look away, but a sharp tug on my chin brings my eyes back to his. He leans in closer, one knee between mine, pinning me in place and hell if I don't feel my panties dampen. Fuck my goddamned body. The grip on my chin tightens.

"Answer, me," he says in warning, his voice at my ear. He'll find a way—elevator, fitting room, backseat of his car—and I'll answer for the way I'm responding if I don't get my shit together. And a part of me wonders if I don't need it, a good session over his knee to help me get rid of this anger and fear simmering inside me.

But not now. Not this way. I take a deep breath and let it out slowly, then nod. And his eyes soften then. He knows that this is taking a lot of effort from me and fuck it *is*. Submitting to him is one of the hardest things I've ever done. How easy would it be for me to tell him to fuck off? To smack my hand against the hard plane of his chest? It's a gazillion times harder to keep my temper in check and *deal*. I take a shuddering breath.

"Yes, sir."

He leans in, and I catch a glimpse of the tattoo that runs along his neck and I know what it leads to, a full back tat with black wings that span his shoulders. I always thought it was hot, so badass. I've always just made assumptions about that tat, but now, I need to know more. Why does he have it? Why hasn't he ever told me the meaning? Why haven't I been willing to take things further so that he'll let me know *more?* Right then, in the moment between fear and obedience, I need more from him.

My phone buzzes. He nods, giving me permission to answer it and for a brief moment my temper flares but I tamp it down again. I can do this. I look at my phone, wondering with a quick slam of my heart against my rib cage that it could be my brother again. But when I look at the screen, I see it's Diana. I show Zack. He raises a brow, and I answer.

"Yeah?"

"Honey, you okay?"

I let out a breath. "I'm actually here, and I even managed to wrangle Zack with me."

I can practically hear her smiling on the phone. "Ha! Sounds good. We're over by the tiaras."

"See you, honey." I shut off my phone and look to Zack.

"They're by the tiaras," I whisper. When his brows furrow in consternation, I huff out a breath. "Do you know what a tiara is?"

He furrows his brow. "Like a crown. Why do you need a princess thing for a wedding?"

And that makes me giggle. "It's a type of crown, yes. Worn for special occasions."

"*Why?*" He looks genuinely baffled. I try not to roll my eyes, as he hates that.

"Come on in, and I'll show you," I say with a smile. He takes my hand, and I feel lighter for a moment. Happier. His hand is warm and reassuring.

We enter the shop, and I glance around, looking for

accessories. I see the sparkle of glittery tiaras in one corner and gently pull his hand, leading him there. Diana waves her hand to me, and I see Tobias beside her, the same pained expression on his face that Zack has. Diana's son, Chad, sits on a chair next to them. He looks up when we come in and I wave to him. He waves, smiles, then looks back down at the book in his hands. We reach them and the guys greet each other with chin lifts. Diana's eyes twinkle, and she holds a gorgeous arrangement of roses in her hand.

"Wow, those are beautiful," I say.

She smiles. "They're for *you*." She looks coyly at Zack. "Trying to out-do Tobias in the romance department, huh?"

But Zack's face is blank. "I didn't send her flowers. What the hell are you talking about?"

Diana's face pales, and Tobias tenses. My stomach suddenly clenches. "Give me the flowers," Zack orders. He reads the tag, and his face is a mask of fury. "Where the hell did these come from?"

Diana shakes her head. "I—I don't know. The salesperson said they were for my party and it's just me and Beatrice, so I looked at the card and didn't ask questions."

Cold washes over me. I feel numb. Exposed. Naked.

Terrified.

I reach for the card and Zack lets me read it as he's already dialing someone on his phone.

To Beatrice, with love.

No signature.

I close my eyes. This isn't happening.

Zack shuts off his phone and shoves it in his pocket, then looks at me. "You'll try on the dress with me in the fucking fitting room with you. You do whatever you've gotta do, then I ask questions. Then we go home."

Chapter 10

Thankfully, Tobias sits next to me in the straight-back, padded chairs they have outside the ladies' fitting rooms because I don't wanna sit here looking at glitter and heels, I want to slam the punching bag at the gym until my muscles ache with pain and sweat blurs my vision. I want to wrap Beatrice up in my arms, carry her home, and then worship every inch of her skin that fucking belongs *to me*. I watched over her as she got changed then took my place out here.

But anger doesn't serve me. Tobias knows this, and he's my friend so he's gonna get what's eating me up without dealing with shit like lengthy conversations.

"What the fuck is going on?" he says under his breath as I watch Beatrice stand on a little pedestal thing and an older woman with huge, round glasses and little metal pins sticking out of her mouth, wraps a measuring tape around her.

I fill him in quickly and I know he gets me when he mutters under his breath, "Motherfucker. She's lucky you let her come here tonight."

"She does *not* need to lose weight," Diana says, her eyes flashing at the lady with the pins and measuring tape. "God, I could weigh her on the produce scale at the supermarket. She's a damn *yoga* instructor and the most beautiful woman I know. We ordered according to your size chart, and it's not her fault it doesn't fit!"

Tobias is already on his feet, Chad blinking in surprise. "Diana," Tobias says warningly, but before Diana says anything else, Beatrice speaks up.

She huffs out a mirthless laugh. "Yeah, no. I know the size I wear, and dieting is not happening. Get me the next size up."

"There's no time!" the woman protests, her lips tight and eyes narrowed. "I'm simply suggesting you cut out a few carbs for the next week, so the zipper *zips.*"

Beatrice's cheeks pink and she points her finger at the woman. I'm watching this, prepared to step in if necessary, but I like that my woman can defend herself. She's submissive to me, and me only, but she can hold her own. "*No.* Order me the next size up."

"There is no *time!*"

"Then we pick out another dress," Diana says. Beatrice looks at her and raises her brow, and I don't know what kinda conversation they're having in silence, but they know each other so well, it happens. There are nods and shrugs and then finally Diana turns to the woman. "The sheath we tried on last time. The off-the-shoulder baby blue one."

"I don't know if that's still in stock," the woman says, and doesn't move. Unbelievable.

Beatrice smiles benevolently. "Oh, that's easily remedied though, isn't it? You just have to go look. Or if you'd prefer me to go to your manager and ask…"

The woman straightens and shakes her head. "That won't be necessary," she says, and she stalks away. Beatrice looks at me and rolls her eyes. Diana and Tobias have a hushed conversation. He comes back to me and sits next to me.

"Our girls can handle shit," he says, a note of pride in his voice. I like that. *Our girls.*

"Damn right they can." I snort. "Diet. I can pick her up with one hand and not even break a sweat."

"I bet."

"Why do you pick her up?" Chad asks, his brows puckering.

Tobias ruffles his hair. "He didn't say he does, he just said he *can*."

Chad frowns, thinks, then nods. "Got it." He goes back to his book.

Tobias fills me in on what's going on at Verge, and I hear a rustling but don't pay attention until I hear Beatrice clear her throat.

I look up and the world fades away from me. The woman found the dress. Beatrice is wearing it, and I'm unprepared for how it makes me feel.

It fits her perfectly, revealing her creamy, shapely shoulders, fitted around her bust, some kinda neckline that makes her look like a princess, the pale blue somehow making her eyes look brighter. She's a vision. A dream.

Fucking *mine.*

I don't even know I'm on my feet until I'm walking to her. "This works for you?" Beatrice asks Diana.

Works for *me.*

I reach out to her and wrap my hand around the back of her neck, right in front of the woman with the measuring tape. She's watching me, but I want her to know this is happening, that she's mine, and if she fucking gives her shit we're done here.

"You look gorgeous, baby," I say, my voice a heated rumble.

Her blue eyes light up like the clouds breaking through the sky on a summer day.

"Then it's done," Diana says, clapping her hands. "*Yes!*"

"Time to go home, *now*," I say.

Beatrice looks at Diana. "But we were going to pick out shoes—"

I shake my head once.

Diana nods. "Go with Zack. He'll keep you safe and find out what's going on. We can get shoes another day," she says quietly. Beatrice gives her a hug, and I go sit down and wait for Beatrice to change again.

"Gotta make that woman yours, man," Tobias says, telling me what I already know

"I know it."

"She won't agree? Still no moving forward?"

I think before I answer. I don't know what her hesitation is. She doesn't come to my place, and though she doesn't date anyone but me, she's not ready to take it to the next level. At least, she hasn't been.

Soon, we need to have a talk.

"Some things happen easily, man," I say. "And then sometimes, you have to build things up." She's holding back, and I don't know why. "Verge has given us trust." Tobias knows it isn't Verge that's brought us to where we are, but what we do there. Every time she obeys me, she steals a little part of me. Every time she drops to her knees, I love her a little more.

My stomach clenches, and I know then. Jesus. *I love her.*

Does she feel the same?

Tobias nods. "Understood. Just wanted to let you know I've got your back."

I nod. "Thanks, brother."

"Officer Williams?" I turn to see a few of the men who work for me coming to collect the flowers. These will be evidence. They'll look into who ordered them, and try to piece shit together.

My job is to take care of my girl.

Beatrice comes out, dressed, and I take her by the hand. Seeing her in that dress made me hard as a rock, and I need to get her home. Need to claim her. She's also way, *way* overdue for a session.

Tonight, I'll fix that.

We drive to my place in silence. There's something palpable between us, but I'm not sure what it is. Is she angry I made her leave? Hell, she was lucky I let her stay. Right now, at this very moment, there's at least one person who's got their eyes set on her and they're a danger to her.

My entire life is dedicated to protecting the lives of those around me. I'll be damned if I let anyone come after *my* woman.

"You're quiet." I break the silence as I navigate the congested streets of NYC, my mind only partly here. The other part of my brain whispers warnings and alerts to me. *Is it the guy on the corner who's staring at us now as he lights up his smoke? The motorcycle I can see in my rear-view mirror that's woven in and out of traffic four times in the past eight blocks? Or is the douchebag sitting at home, enjoying cyberstalking, laughing in the knowledge he's fucked her up and pissed me off? Or is it a she?*

I realize she's said something and I feel like a douchebag because I have no idea what she's just said. She exhales and looks out the window. "Not that it matters."

"Not that what matters?"

She turns to me with an impatient flick of her wrist. "God, Zack. Did you even hear a word I said?"

"Watch that tone," I snap.

Yeah, she so fucking needs a session.

She huffs out a breath. "Sorry."

"I'm sorry, too, babe. I'm distracted. Someone's fucking around with you and it pisses me off."

"Doesn't exactly make me happy, either."

I reach for her leg and place my hand on her knee with a gentle squeeze, a two-fold reminder that I've got her, and she needs to watch her temper.

"Doll." I say nothing more at first, just letting the weight of my name for her settle. Calm her.

"Yes?" She finally says in a softer tone, then modifies, "Yes, sir?" Good. She's getting into her submissive head-space. It takes effort for her to get there, but she knows as well as I do how much she needs this tonight. Beatrice bows to *no one* but me, and I get a fucking hard-on just thinking about that. Christ, how I love her submission to me.

"You listen to me. I'm going to do everything I can to find who's pulling this shit. But I'm going to ask you to do some shit you're not gonna like."

She tenses but keeps her voice in check. "Oh?"

"Yeah. And there's one thing you need to know. You have to trust me. I've got this. I'm going to keep you safe. But baby, you've got to *trust* me."

She doesn't say anything for a moment, and then finally she says in a low, somewhat shaky voice, "I do."

Does she? She trusts me to tie her up and spank her ass. She trusts me to snap my collar on her neck and dole out measured pain under the firmness of my hand. But until recently, there was shit about her I didn't know. And this is the first night she's sleeping at my place. What exactly does trust mean to her?

"More, Bea. I need more trust from you. Not just scening. Not just obedience. I need you to trust me with *you.*"

She doesn't respond. It's okay. I'm not looking for a response. I need her to think about it.

She lays her hand in mine, and I can smell lilies and lemons. Heat and desire curls in my gut as I take the final turn that leads to my place.

Maybe building her trust needs to happen where we are. Maybe scening is how I reach her, how I break down those walls. How I make her really, *truly* mine.

It's time to ratchet things up.

"You need to let go tonight, Beatrice." And fuck, so do I.

Her voice is taut with heat and need. "Yes, sir," she purrs, and then her voice is a plea that hits me in the solar plexus. "*Please*, sir." The vision of her on her knees, blind-folded, hands restrained behind her back as she chokes on my cock makes blood thrum through my body, course through my veins, my dick lengthening.

I'll do a run-through of my place when we get there, and if the fucker has the nerve to come to my turf, I'll fucking *kill* him. Tonight, I'll give her what she needs. What we *both* need. Tomorrow, I get shit in place to keep her safe.

I swerve into my designated spot, cut the engine. "Stay there."

If anyone out there's tailed us, I want them to see me, to see how much I care about her, so they know, they touch a fucking hair on her head and I'll end them.

I open her door, help her out, and the second I do, my hand is on the small of her back, guiding her to the entrance, my body shielding her from the street and crowds as we go straight to the elevator.

"Williams." A neighbor lifts his chin in greeting and I grunt one in return, walking her with wide, purposeful steps. The entryway door shuts behind us and my hand goes to her neck, wrapping my fingers at the back of her head to both claim and soothe. The mirrored elevator slides open, and a couple comes out, the man's eyes going to Beatrice. I don't recognize him, but he nods at me, the woman's focus somewhere else. Immediately, I'm on edge. Is it him? Is he the one tailing her? They leave and the door shuts, closing us in alone.

"You tense whenever anyone looks at me, Zack," she says. Damn, she's right. People look at her all the time. She's funny and beautiful and sweet and smart. Why wouldn't they?

I shake my head. "I hate what's gone down, and I can't help it. I won't rest until they're behind bars."

She places her hand on my arm. "They will be, baby."

She's the one soothing me? This is fucked up. I take in a deep breath. She doesn't need to see me lose my shit. I didn't end up a detective and dom by wearing my heart on my sleeve, like some half-cocked bastard with an axe to grind.

Control.

Focus.

Patience.

I open the door to my condo, shut it, and in one swift move, pin her against it, her wrists in my hands above her head, my body pressed up against hers. I lean in and take her mouth hard, running my tongue along hers, then nipping her bottom lip lightly before I pull back, leaving her breathless.

"You stay right here," I command in her ear. My place is tighter than a fucking vault, but I do a quick scan anyway, come back, and shrug off my jacket. She's still frozen in place, her eyes bright like they always are before we scene.

"I'll give you the tour later. Bedroom's last door on the

right. I'm taking care of some business and I'll be in there as soon as I can." I keep my eyes locked on hers and command, "Go to my room. Strip. Present for me. And keep your eyes closed. Focus, baby. Prepare yourself for me."

Her eyes gleam with arousal and excitement and just a little of the worry disappears from her expression. She doesn't respond at first. Testing me? I cross the room, take her by the arm, spin her around, and give her a sharp smack to the ass. "I said *go.*"

"Yes, sir!"

I send her to the room with another crisp spank, then watch her go, hands adorably rubbing her ass as she makes her way to my room. Her head flits from side to side as she tries to take it all in on her way and I can hardly contain my laughter. Damn, she's adorable.

The door shuts with a soft click.

I pull out my cell and dial.

"Yeah? What's up, Williams?"

I fill Patel in on what's happened today. He shares my concern, and we make an easy plan to get at least one man on Beatrice at all times. I'll escort her to and from where she's gotta go, but we can put more in place for when I'm not there.

"She knows you're doing this?"

A twinge of guilt makes me pause before I respond. Frowning, I look behind me at the door, then walk to the furthest corner of the room, staring at my dim reflection in the large flat-screened TV hung suspended on the wall, opposite the leather wrap-around couch. I keep my voice low.

"*No.*" It comes out sharper than I intend.

I hear him blow out a breath. "Why not?"

Why not? I don't want to piss her off. I don't want her to feel even more exposed than she already does.

"I'll tell her, Patel, just not yet." I'll fill her in when the time is right. I shove down the guilt that nags at me. I have to do this for her. We make plans, then I disconnect the call, close my eyes and inhale deeply. I can't shut off my brain. It pieces things together no matter where I am or what I do. I notice details, minor things others might overlook.

I rub my fingers along the scruff of my jaw, contemplating, when I hear a creak on the bed in my room. I can't leave her alone like this. Now is not the time to be the detective. Now, my woman needs me. Her dom.

I turn to the door and throw the deadbolt in place with a heavy *thunk*. I go to the shades and draw them down, then shut off all the lights. The fucker might be out there, but he'll see nothing. Then I make my way to the room where she's waiting, my mind still spinning every detail of what I've heard.

He moved the car. Therefore, he… or *she*… was in her salon and either got her keys or got a copy of *my* keys which seems totally preposterous. She doesn't keep an eye on her bag, so that's the more likely possibility.

They left a card on the seat. Who? Why?

The first card she got was at the wedding and that started everything going… I open the door to the room, and my mind comes to a screeching halt.

In front of me lies absolute *perfection*. My world stops, my breath catches in my throat, and it's all I can do not to fall at her feet and fucking venerate her. She's done exactly what I've asked. Her clothes are neatly folded and on the edge of the bed, and she's naked, her pale skin a canvas, waiting for me to color. Soft, wavy blonde hair falls over her shoulders, her head tipped to the side, golden satin I want to stroke. Her eyes are closed, and her body softly lifts and falls, her breathing slow and steady. I wanted this for her. Relaxation under my command. The exchange of power we both crave.

I stand in the doorway and watch her a little longer, knowing the anticipation will build for her. If I touch her, she'll be primed for me, ready. And training her to wait for me works to my benefit.

If I were an artist, I'd spend night and day painting this until I captured every curve, the strength in her submission, the beauty of what she's freely giving to me.

Wars were fought over women like her.

Hell, I'm fighting one now.

I walk over slowly to the bed, stripping, and I can see she wants to open her eyes by the way she struggles a bit, shifting on the bed.

"You may open your eyes for now," I allow, only because I need to see the baby blues that stole my heart. Her long lashes flutter open, and she looks at me, smiling. She watches me strip without apology, her eyes roaming my body, lingering on my tattoos, and I know that when I bend to slip my pants from my feet, she will take in the marks along my back, the tattooed wings, and the scar, symbols of my past I've not shared with her. Why haven't I? I want more from her. I'm tired of the linear progression of our relationship. She's adorable and sweet, sexy as fuck, brilliant... and submissive to me. I want this to be my forever—her, me, *us*. I've always been the kinda guy who wanted more. Connection. A relationship with meaning and purpose. And she's holding back.

Am I?

I need to know why.

But tonight, I need to erase the fears of the day from

her mind. I need to remind her who I am, who she is, and that she obeys me. It's for her own good.

When I'm stripped to my boxers, I step over to her, lean down, and caress her soft, silky hair. Her eyelids quickly flutter shut and her back rises as she takes in a breath. I weave the gold around my fingers, mesmerized by the contrast of her light hair against the darker skin of my hand. My fingers entwined in her hair, I pull her head back sharply, a tug that makes her gasp in pain, jolting her into her place. I gently release her hair and wrap my fingers first around the back of her neck, massaging the tension there. Pain and pleasure, sprinkled with fear and laden with ecstasy, a slow build-up of emotion and sensations that will bring her where I want her.

Soaring.

Malleable.

Mine.

I move my fingers from the back of her neck around to her throat, feeling her swallow through the thin, vulnerable skin, my palm pressed against her as she draws and releases breath. Slowly, deliberately, I squeeze, just enough to bring her heartbeat up, her pulse quickening against my skin. My whole hand wrapped around her throat, I marvel at the well of trust she gives me.

My job has not been an easy one. I've hurt, punished, and maimed with my hands. I could hurt her now if I wanted to, and a part of me does. The temptation to abuse the power she gives me lurks in the shadows, whispering *hurt her. Make her cry. Show her your power and strength.* But I bat it away. I've learned to master the sinister part of me and replace it with sensual sadism. With a sharp release of breath, I'm in control once more. I'm stronger than temptation.

She breathes in and out, at peace with the dangerous

grip I have on her. She struggles with giving me the power. I struggle with wielding it. We both war with the exchange of power. It's in the mutual yielding we grow our trust.

A gentler flex on her throat, and then I release her altogether, not touching her at all. I brace myself on the bed, lean down, and gently blow air across her back. She shivers. I lean down and kiss her shoulder, then move her hair off her neck and kiss her there before I slowly draw my tongue down the length of her spine, savoring the sweet, salty taste of her skin. When she arches, I slip my hand under the space between the bed and her belly, bracing her. When I reach the small of her back, I suck her flesh in my mouth, only releasing when I've marked her with a pink circle. There is only one place of her body sweeter than this.

I'll get there.

I release her. She falls back to the bed with a whimper. I give her ass a sharp, approving spank, the sound echoing in the room, and she moans.

"Please, sir," she whispers, and her voice shakes. "Bring me there."

No further words are needed. I know what she needs from me. I lean in and kiss the sensitive skin just below her ear.

I whisper in her ear, the vibration in tune with the tenderness she evokes in me.

"You need release, doll."

Her eyes are still shut, her chin quivering. Other women would need something else. A hug. A shot. Some time alone. But not Beatrice. She needs more than that.

I whisper against the shell of her ear. "You need me to help you let this go," I whisper. "Take the pain away tonight."

A lone tear slides down her cheek and to her chin.

I lean down and capture it with my tongue, empowered with the salty taste of it. It belongs to me now, her hurt and fears. Her trust.

"Make me hurt," she whispers, a plea. And in that moment, I'd give her anything. I'd planned on keeping her on the bed in my favorite position for her, presenting herself to me, giving me full access to her full backside and most sensitive parts, but she needs something different tonight. She'll need me to restrain her.

I move over to the bed and hear her shuddering breath once more. Sweet girl, she's barely restraining her need to cry. I open the drawer next to my bed and take out what I need. Her lids flutter open, shining with tears, and go wide at the sight of the lengths of leather lashes bound with the long, heavy handle.

"Close your eyes, Beatrice." I could blindfold her, but I want her to make the choice. "If you open your eyes again without permission, I'll punish you."

Her eyes shut tight.

I lay the flogger next to her on the bed, and take out a coil of satin binding, then a stout wooden paddle. Her brows draw together and her lips thin as she listens to me moving around. It's rectangular, varnished, and unyielding. The element of surprise will work in my favor tonight.

I unfurl the satin, lean over her and wrap it around her wrists. Her eyes stay shut. "Good girl," I whisper. She stiffens, but I ignore that. She's taut, her whole body wound, but that's okay. I need her to snap. She can't let go until she does.

I lift the flogger and trail the soft tails along her shoulders. She whimpers, knowing this is only a prelude to what will come. I tickle her back, her ass, the tops of her thighs and all the way to her feet. "Let it all go, Beatrice," I say.

Once I begin, the pain will be her focus. Pain, and obedience.

"Yes, sir."

I lift the flogger and bring it down with moderate force. The leather lashes strike her bare skin once, twice, three times. I ignore her cries and place my hand on her lower back to hold her in place, then flick my wrist to the left, then right, whipping every inch of her until her skin is reddened and primed. I pause, hold the lashes in my hand, and slide the handle between her legs. She chokes on a cry of surprise as I tease her clit with the handle. It slides easily in her slick folds, then I draw it back, still holding the lashes, and strike her hard with the crop-like handle. I pause between smacks of the handle, the swish and thud making her squirm and moan.

"Ow, sir," she pleads. "Stop. Oh, God, that hurts."

She doesn't mean stop, though. She has a safeword, and *stop* isn't it. She has to say this. She needs to beg me to stop. She needs to know I won't. If I stop now, she's in charge, and she needs *me* to control this.

"Behave yourself," I growl.

She arches her back and pushes up onto her palms. "No!" Her voice is a garbled mixture of emotions. Tears run freely down her cheeks. I slap her ass and push her back down onto her chest. I'm not angered by her defiance. It's natural to push a little. I bring back the flogger and give her three rapid, wicked lashes, criss-crossed tiny welts raising along her skin. I drop the flogger, raise my palm, then smack my hand, hard, against her ass.

"Chest down," I bark. "Speak again without permission and you know what happens." Punishment could be anything I choose. I spank her with my palm once more. I've got an arsenal of implements at my disposal, but I need the flesh-on-flesh contact, and so does she.

She quietly weeps into the bed, but I'm not the one making her cry. This is what she needs, this cathartic release.

I reach for the paddle, hold it firmly in my grip, and whack the underside of her thighs. She screams in surprise, but I don't give her time to settle. I spank her again, and again. My stomach clenches and my cock lengthens. I could take her right here, right now, but she needs more. I paddle her with firm, deliberate strokes, alternating where and how I strike her. She's crying softly now, but she no longer flinches with the smack of the paddle. She's primed, floating into her submission, the place where I can take her deeper and further away from her pain. I give her another, harsher stroke, and she barely moves. A second, and a third. Minutes pass, and the only sound is the smack of wood on skin and her heavy breathing.

I place the paddle down on the bed and massage her inflamed skin. She hisses at the touch of my palm raking across her punished ass. I pat her rounded bottom in approval. "Stay there," I instruct, moving back to the drawer and taking out a riding crop. This will be practically play after what she's taken, but it's the varied sensation she needs tonight.

One snap of the crop and she moans, a second, and she whimpers. One after the other, I lay stripes across her ass, the little square of leather marking her already pink skin. Rounds with the crop give way to another with the flogger, then another with the paddle. Time ticks on and I'm careful not to hurt her, never striking her lower back, watching the rise of color carefully. Sweat breaks out along my brow, and I'm panting from the exertion. I've primed her well enough not to hurt her. It's a thorough session she'll feel, but she won't be harmed.

"You're brave, doll," I approve, running my hand along my artwork.

She mumbles something incoherent. It's what I want to hear, a signal to me she's entering subspace.

This is where I take complete control.

Chapter 11

I could weep with thanksgiving. Hell, I think I might be. I feel something split wide open in my chest and the dark emotions that have held me in bondage break apart when the pain permeates my entire being. I crave this, but I fight it. I have to. Even when I screamed and pled with him to stop, he kept on, beating my ass, my bruised and welted skin tame compared to the ache I feel in my heart and chest. I'm not even sure I want anything else but to crawl up on his chest and soak in every bit of the aftercare he gives me. I can't think. My mind is swirls and colors and jumbled thoughts I can't hold, but I embrace this freedom.

Sometimes I need to feel pain to bear it.

Free. Flying. I'm *flying*.

"Baby," I hear but he's speaking in a tunnel somewhere in the distance. I nod, needing more somehow, and when I feel his fingers plunge in my core I know *yes*. I need that final closure on my release. He lifts me in his arms and kisses me fiercely, the prickle of the whiskers that line his mouth sharp and tingly, his hold strong, his skin damp with perspiration. He places me down on a pile of pillows, and my eyes close, enveloped in his strength, his scent, his command.

"God, I wanna fuck you," he growls in my ear. "But ladies first."

He props my scorched ass up with a pillow, then bends down, drawing my hardened nipple into his mouth.

Yes. God, yes.

His powerful tongue laves at the sensitive bud, then suckles and nips. I'm flying. *Soaring.* Seconds ago, all I could feel was euphoria, but at the feel of his hands on me I need *so much more.* He releases my breasts and moves along the bed, leans his beautiful body down, and lifts my pussy to his mouth.

Please, my mind begs, but I can't say anything, my body almost completely out of my control. His scratchy whiskers scrape along the sensitive skin of my inner thighs, and *God,* I fucking love it, just before he pulls my clit into his mouth with a fierce suckling. I buck and writhe, and he eats me out until my body tenses and I writhe beneath him, He pins me down, rakes his tongue up the length of my slit once, twice, and I'm so primed, at the third stroke, I shatter.

The power of my climax is so hard it almost hurts, every muscle spasming while ecstasy courses through me. I can't speak.

Zack.

I love you.

I climax so hard and long it feels never-ending until I finally collapse. He's on top of me, then, holding his large, muscular frame just barely controlled over mine. "Fucked you with my mouth," he says in my ear. "Need to take this pussy. Jesus, doll, watching you come like that almost made me lose control." He quickly unfastens the bindings at my wrists.

I beam at him, though I can't talk. *Almost.* He won't actually lose control.

I spread my legs wide, smiling in anticipation of being filled by him. He holds himself just at my entrance, captures my wrists, and his mouth kisses my neck at the same moment he plunges into me. He thrusts and moans and I rise to meet him, sated now that I'm being filled by him. My master. My sir. *My love.* Frenzied, rapid pulses between my legs and he's grunting, groaning, then the deep growl emanates from deep within me as he climaxes. He releases my wrists and without thought, my arms encircle his neck and his forehead drops to mine. No one understands what I need like he does.

He pulls out of me and I know he does something to clean me up, but I don't know how he does it or how long he's gone, I just know that I'm clean, marked, naked.

Safe.

He climbs into bed and holds a cup of water to my mouth. I start shivering, and he pulls me up to the side of his chest, my skin flush against his, the little hairs on his chest tickling me, and his arms wrap around me. I crook one knee up, my arm draped around the expanse of his chest, and kiss whichever part of him I can reach. His chest, his shoulder, and then my eyes are too heavy to keep open. I float, drifting off into a dreamless sleep.

I WAKE the next morning and find myself wrapped all up in Zack. Our legs are entangled, my hair all over the place, and his eyes are still closed. Is he awake?

There's one way to tell. I slide my hand under the blanket until I can find his cock, ramrod straight and ready for action. I giggle.

"Come out, come out, wherever you are," I whisper. "Come on, buddy. I wanna play."

His lips quirk up and he snorts, his voice gritty with sleep as he rumbles, "Did you just seriously call my dick buddy?"

"He's my best friend," I murmur sleepily, squealing as his hand snakes down and gives my ass a punishing squeeze.

"Oh shit am I sore. *Shiiiiiit.* God, you worked me over good."

He opens one eye and nods. "Mhm." He sobers. "You needed it." I remember, then, why, and a touch of my post-subspace bliss vanishes.

"I did," I whisper. "Any news today?"

He shakes his head. "Haven't gotten me and my *buddy* out of bed yet," he says, and though his lips twitch, his eyes are more serious.

"What time is it?"

"Time for a round two," he says, rolling me over. Good thing I'm naked, because it sure as hell makes things a little quicker. He's in me already, and my ass screams a protest against his soft sheets, but it feels so good to have him in me like this that I'm already pulsing with need, my breasts swelling, and in record time, we both topple into climax, bedhead and all.

"Mmm, tiger," I say, running my purple fingernails along his back. "You've got quite the appetite." His body weight presses against me. God, it feels good, like the comfort of a weighted blanket, and his head nuzzles against my breasts. I twirl my fingers in his soft brown hair and I can't help but give it a little tug.

"You may've just fucked me boneless, but I'm still your dom, brat," he growls.

I bite my lip and my heart flutters.

My dom. My boyfriend. He wants more than that, though.

To so many right now, he's my fiancé.

Why can't he be that to me?

"Yes, sir," I say. I run my fingers along his scalp, gently at first, then weaving through the thick, honey-colored hair, then down to his neck. He sighs, and my hands go to his shoulders, tracing along the edges of the stark black tattooed wings that spread along his back.

"What does your tattoo mean?" I whisper. He has many, but this is the one I want to know about. I feel his whole body tense atop mine. Then he breathes in deep and lets out a deep, shuddering breath.

"I got that tat on my eighteenth birthday." In my mind's eye I envision Zack, with the same deep brown eyes and serious-stern expression on his face, maybe totally clean-shaven and a little slimmer than he is now. I've asked him about the tattoos before, and he's always shrugged and told me he'd explain some day. It seems that day is now. I listen reverently, knowing that somehow this moment is sacred.

"It's in memory of my older sister."

I open my mouth and almost speak what immediately comes to my mind. He has one sister, Tia, and she's younger than he is. He doesn't have two sisters. But thankfully, reality dawns a split second later and I realize what he's saying. I close my eyes briefly, a lump forming in my throat, then flutter my lids open. If he's brave enough to tell me, I'm brave enough to listen.

"She died my senior year in high school."

"Zack," I whisper. My voice is ragged, not asking for anything, but telling him I'm here. I'm listening.

"She got involved with the wrong crowd. My parents knew she was doing shit she shouldn't be when she was a junior, and they tried to get involved, but they're older. They didn't get married until later in life, so by the time they had us, they were already much older than most other parents who had teens. So anyway, when Alicia told them she wasn't doing anything wrong, they believed her. Well, I knew better. But what could I do? I was her kid brother."

He lifts his head from my chest and lays both hands beneath his chin, still resting on me, the beautiful expanse of his muscled shoulders reminding me he's all man, but the boy who lost his sister still kindles in his eyes. "Her boyfriend was into drugs, just pot at first. His friends were into heavier shit. When she began college, she partied on the weekends, and by then she was too far gone. She OD'd." He looks away for a minute and I watch as his Adam's apple bobs. His voice comes out in a hoarse whisper. "I was the one that found her. I went out looking for her when she didn't come home one night, and my mother was frantic. She'd been trying to make it home, they think. But she didn't."

I don't try to wipe away the tears that fall unchecked. I can picture her, a feminine version of the man now in front of me, long hair, and those beautiful brown eyes framed with longer lashes.

He takes in another shuddering breath. "So, on my eighteenth birthday, I got this tat. Wings for Alicia. Her initials scrolled underneath." He chuckles. "My mom was furious. Thinks tats are some kinda mark of the devil." He shrugs. "My dad, he got it." He pauses, and his brows draw together. "Never told anyone before."

"Why not?" I ask.

He looks to me with a sad smile on his lips. "No one's ever asked, until you."

He puts his hand on my chest again and I *squeeze* him, so hard it almost hurts. He looks up at me and his eyes grow serious. "Beatrice. I've wanted to take things deeper with you for a while."

"I know," I whisper.

He reaches his fingers to my chin, his index finger lifting it up just enough so I can't look away. "It's time, doll."

I have no words and can only nod. His phone rings, a ringtone I've never heard before, and he knifes up in the bed.

"Need to take that." And he's gone, pulling on a pair of boxers with one hand while grabbing his phone with the other, and I watch as he leaves the room. I can't hear a word he's saying, and I want to, but as I push myself up in bed, the only thing I feel right now is pain. He's whipped me good, two days in a row, but for some reason I love it. I close my eyes and slide back down on his sheets, feeling the deep throb in my ass, similar to the familiar, rewarding ache I get after I've worked out hard at the gym.

He's marked me as his.

I look around his room while I hear him talking in the other room, his voice rising and falling. He seems a little angry about something, but he's a detective, so I know there are things that get under his skin from time to time.

How can I have been with him for so long and never been here before? It isn't because he hasn't asked me. But until very recently… I simply wasn't ready. Not ready to let down my walls and show him who I really am, and my entire life I was the spoiled princess. It wasn't until college that I realized *no*, it wasn't who I was, I would not marry some rich, pompous asshole or even a rich nice guy. I never could decipher who wanted me for money, so when I went off on my own I was determined I would be *me*. Beatrice Ann Moore. Yoga instructor, loyal friend, and hairdresser extraordinaire.

But getting closer to Zack scares me. He's all in with the lifestyle, and I'm not so sure. It's hot as fucking hell. I love to scene with him. But beyond that? Is it *me?*

I sigh, taking in the very manly, fairly utilitarian look of the place. There are no picture frames or even prints on the wall. He doesn't even have so much as curtains on his window. The walls are a plain cream color, the floors hard-wood save a handful of throw rugs in burgundy and hunter green. The large dresser against one wall is simple but sturdy, and he has a variety of things on top, but it doesn't look cluttered, just practical. I know he took out imple-ments next to his bed, and I want to open that drawer, but it feels like a violation of his privacy.

Still… He spanks my ass and I wear his collar and crawl to him. I can't look in his drawers? My hand goes to the handle, and I gently tug it open so it makes no noise. I gasp when I see the contents.

To one side he has things I'm very familiar with. The flogger, a cane, a variety of paddles and whips, and a sturdy strap. Nipple clamps and lube, and other things he packs and takes with him to Verge. Condoms. But gleaming silver catches my eye, and I push the kinky mountain aside to get a better look. It's a revolver, a pair of handcuffs, and a lockbox.

Shit. This drawer's frigging explosive. Like, literally. I shut it so fast it slams with a bang, and I cringe as I hear the door to his room swing open.

"Beatrice."

"Yes, sir?" Maybe tacking on the sir will help my case. I can't look at him, but the tone of his voice makes my skin prickle.

"Were you snooping in my drawers?"

I turn to him and shake my head. "No, sir. You weren't wearing any drawers this morning. I fucked you naked and don't need to snoop since I know every intimate detail of your—"

"*Beatrice*." His voice is the warning tone, the old-man lecture voice. He's all Stern Dom.

I sigh. "Yes. I knew you kept the fun play things in there." My voice drops. "I just... I just didn't know you kept other things in there, too."

I finally hazard a look up at him, and his brown eyes have darkened to nearly black, his jaw tight, hands on his hips. Fuck, he's gorgeous when he's stern. And *really* intimidating. I suddenly feel about six years old.

He reaches me and sits on the edge of the bed. I roll over on my side to face him, tucking my hands beneath my cheek, which was a mistake, since now that he can reach me, he gives my ass a firm swat.

"Ow! I'm sore you know."

"I'm sure," he says, raising a brow at me. "Which is the only reason I'm not taking you across my lap for snooping. I have nothing to hide from you. *Nothing.*"

Guilt gnaws at my gut.

"But I don't like that you didn't just ask me but felt the need to sneak."

"You weren't here."

He crosses his arms and his eyes narrow.

I sigh. "I'm sorry. You're right. I shouldn't have snooped."

He threads his fingers through my hair, and his voice softens a bit. "There are dangerous things in that drawer. Things that could hurt little girls who aren't careful."

"I'm not your little girl," I say, even though I sort of love when he calls me that.

"No?" he asks.

I shake my head but it's sheer petulance. I love being taken care of. He opens the drawer, reaches in, and takes out something I didn't see before—a sturdy wooden hair-brush. The breath catches in my throat and I wonder for a moment if he's going to spank me. I mean, nearly all the other tools in there are implements of ass destruction. But no, instead, he gently draws the brush through my hair. "Sit up," he instructs gently. I obey, and he pulls me to him, swinging his legs up on the bed so I can lean against his torso, while he brushes my hair. Bending down to whisper in my ear, he asks, "Are you sure you don't like being my little girl?"

Oh, I fucking love this.

I don't know what to say, so I don't say anything.

He just chuckles. He knows I fight this.

"Beatrice."

"Yes?"

"You're staying here until further notice. You got that?"

He isn't offering or inviting me, but *telling* me, and at first a spark of anger flares to life in my chest. Who does he think he is? I didn't tell him I'd move in with him. Is this some sorta power play? But I've resisted for *so long,* and I don't feel ready at *all* to go back to my place. No, thank you, not now, not when some kinda shit's going down. So I swallow my pride and nod.

"Did you find out anything about the flowers dropped off?"

"All anonymous, and it was a fake name and cash at the ordering place. No records."

"Well, that just sucks monkey balls." I frown.

I can feel him shaking with laughter. "It isn't funny, but sometimes, the shit you say—"

My phone rings, and I reach for it. "It's Diana," I explain, before I pick it up.

"Make it quick because we've got to talk."

I nod, and answer the phone. "Yeah, babe?"

"Hey, how are you?"

"Doing great," I say, still feeling the residual euphoria from subspace the night before.

She giggles. "Well, then. We need a girl chat later, methinks."

"Pfft. Like I kiss and tell."

She laughs out loud. "So it's totally fine for *me* to give you every juicy detail of my sex life and kinky adventures, but suddenly you're all quiet? Yeah, chickie, I don't think so."

Zack makes a grumbly noise from where he's sitting, and he has the nerve to take the brush in his hand and smack the back of it against his palm. I may not be fully trained but *that's* enough to make me snap into shape.

"Hey, Zack needs to talk to me, I have to make this quick. What's up?"

"Gotta test out cake samples later but Tobias has some meeting or something and he says he doesn't like cake anyway."

"Who doesn't like cake?"

Another smack on Zack's palm has me stuttering. "Ok, ok, when and where?" I get the details from her. "I'll be there."

"Thanks, babe. Later."

We disconnect.

I'm proud of myself for hanging up so quickly when conversations with Diana can sometimes be epic, and we haven't had a really good gab in a while. So I take a minute to swipe at the notifications on my phone, and don't look at Zack, but then I jump when the phone is taken right out of my hand and when I look up in surprise, he's glaring at me.

"Dude. What?"

"Let's try *sir* again," he bites out.

What?

"Excuse me?"

He takes in a deep breath and lets it out slowly. "You want your phone back today? Then watch your fucking attitude and tell me why you just made *plans* without discussing it with me? When I want to fucking keep you here and lock you in a cage to keep you *away* from whoever wants to hurt you? Just, *yeah*, go buy shoes or whatever with Diana? Jesus, if you weren't already marked I'd spank your ass."

My temper flares and I want to mouth off. Buy shoes? Cage? What the *hell* has crawled up his ass? But I reach down deep, take a deep breath, and let it out slowly. I don't want to fight him. I *know* I can keep my temper in check, and I sure as hell don't want to be punished.

"Yes, sir." It's barely meek, and it isn't snarky, but swallowing my anger makes me emotional. Tears cloud my vision. I blink them back, and my voice is shaky, my nose tingling when I ask in a voice barely above a whisper, "Why are you angry with me?"

It's my kryptonite, the chink in my armor.

I hate when I'm the bad girl. I fuck everything up.

Can't you do anything right? The inner voice in my head chides me. I turn my head away from him since I don't want him to see me cry.

"Fuck, baby." His voice is tortured, and then he's got me in his arms, pulling me to his chest, and shit, I'm crying.

"I didn't mean to mess anything up," I sniffle. "God, Zack, I don't want you mad at me. I just didn't think. And I know you want me safe, but I—"

"No, babe, Shhh. God, I'm a dick."

He holds me tight and I do my best to get my shit together. I take a deep breath and let it out, but wetness dampens my cheeks and his chest. We say nothing at first, and then I lift my head. "So I should've asked you first. I just wasn't thinking, honest."

His arms tighten around me. "I just want to keep you safe. I don't like not knowing what's going on, Beatrice. But it isn't fair for me to take that out on you. And I'm sorry. Forgive me?"

He's as demanding as they come but has the balls to swallow his pride and apologize.

"Of course, I forgive you," I sniffle, and he holds me quietly for a moment. "But you may have to make it up to me."

"Yeah?" There's humor in his voice, which pleases me. "Jesus, I could fuck you all day and make you come a thousand times til Sunday and you'll still want more."

"Is sex all you think about?" I tease.

He loosens his grip and tickles me, making me scream and giggle. "No. God, no!" I gasp. "I want a caramel latte with the foamy stuff on top and sprinkles."

"Foamy stuffy?" He shakes. "Tell you what. I can make you one right here."

I pull away from him and look at him quizzically.

"Who can make caramel lattes with foamy stuff and sprinkles by *themselves?*"

He grins, and God, my insides *melt*. So. Damn. Hot.

"Okay," he allows. "Maybe not the sprinkles." His brow furrows, and it's adorable. "But I love making coffee stuff at home. I've got all the equipment and machines, and don't like buying them because they don't make them the way I like them when I do."

Leave it to Zack to Dom his coffee.

"This I've gotta see."

"Whoa, now, doll," he says, grabbing my legs as the swing off the bed, and placing them gently back on the bed. "First, we talk. I have questions for you, but some will wait. All I need to know for now is what your plans are for the next few days. Work hours. Classes you're teaching. Plans with Diana?"

I nod. "Yes, sir, but I'll need my phone." Now it feels nice to call him sir again, and I need to if I'm asking permission for my phone back.

He hands it to me silently, and I swipe my calendar open. "Well I know I don't have to teach yoga this week, because the studio's being renovated. Bonus, I get paid anyway." I frown and look at him. "I need to get my exercise in, though."

"Got plenty of stuff here for you to work out." A corner of his mouth tips up. "And I can work you out good, too."

I shift on my ass and feel the burn. "That you do, sir." God, I want to go back to the club. "Can we go to Verge this weekend?"

His eyes burn. "Hell yeah. But back to your schedule."

"Okay, I have to go with Diana to taste test cake." I pause and amend, "if that's okay with you?"

"Yes, that's fine. Work?"

"No more shifts until next week."

"Perfect." He smiles. "Then I've got you to myself this weekend." He gives my hair a little tug. "Up and at 'em. Go get ready, and I'll make you your fancy pants coffee, then I'll escort you to meet Diana. There's a bag in my living room with clothes I had one of my guys pick up for you."

He leans down and gently kisses my temple, then stands up and gives my ass a smack so hard the noise rings in my ears. I squeal, but I'd be lying if I said I didn't like it.

Chapter 12

I make her coffee while she showers, adding the caramel and swirls and foam like she wants. I normally like my coffee made from freshly-ground beans, straight up with cream, but I've got a sweet tooth and sometimes I want it all doctored up. I don't think I have *sprinkles*, but then I remember in the summer, Tia came over with her daughter for her birthday and for dessert we had all the sundae fixings. Were there sprinkles or some shit like that? I rifle through my cabinets and *boom*. Chocolate sprinkles. I smirk.

God, what I do for this girl.

But as I swirl her coffee and tap the sprinkles on top, guilt tugs at my conscience. I just lectured the hell outta her and brought her to tears for not being straight with me, and just this morning while she still laid in bed, I put plans in place to have a man on her in my absence. She doesn't know she's going to be tailed. Doesn't know I've got her phone tapped. I don't want to freak her out, but I'm not totally at ease with what some might call a double standard.

"Oh that looks awesome," she says, practically skipping over to me. She looks like a little sprite, her blonde hair damp and a little crazy, wearing a pair of tight-fitting jeans that hug her ass, paired with a light blue tank-top, her bare feet revealing bright pink toenails. Her skin is pink and fresh, no makeup yet.

"Where you going, looking so good?" I ask, not bothering to temper my growl.

She starts to roll her eyes but stops and composes herself. "Sweetie," she says with patience, "I'm wearing *jeans and a tank top*. Like, I don't even have makeup on."

I push her cappuccino to her on the counter, reach for her, and drag her over to me, tucking my fingers around her neck just before I claim her with my mouth. She rises into me on the tips of her toes and I don't let her go until she's breathless.

She blinks at me, a little dazzled, and I leave her to go get ready. After I'm showered and dressed, I reach for my drawer and take out my Colt, the smallest handgun I carry with me when there's imminent danger. Beatrice walks in.

"God, Zack!"

I turn to look at her, but her eyes are on the assortment of guns I've got laid out on the bed. Before I chose the one I needed I inspected a few that have been there a while, making sure they are in good condition and loaded.

"Why do you have so many? Why don't you just need one?"

I shrug. "You only have one hair comb?"

"Well, no."

"Only got one pair of scissors?"

She shakes her head. "No, and I know where you're going with this, but that isn't the same. Scissors don't *kill* people. I mean they *can*," she says with a cringe, looking as if she's just eaten something rotten, like in that episode in

126

Sons of Anarchy when she just *rammed*—Oh, God, I can't *even*. That was horrific."

"*Beatrice*." She stops and blinks, but I give her no further instructions, just calling her name in the voice that gets her attention. I inhale deeply. She's adorable but needs to listen to me. I've stepped things up at the club, and she obeys me, but when we're not there, she loses her focus. It's not a command to kneel, this time. It's a command to *focus*. I crook a finger to have her come near. She walks over to me on unsteady feet, as if wondering what I'll do to her when she's near, but when she does, I just take her by the chin and lift her eyes to mine.

"This is who I am. I'm the guy that protects people. I carry weapons. I try my *damndest* not to use them, but babe, if I need to, I *will*."

She swallows and tries to nod but it's hard with my grip on her chin. "Okay," she whispers. "But I really hope you don't need to."

I let her chin go and finish getting dressed. She surprises me when she snickers so I look over her.

"I don't know, officer," she says with the goofiest voice. "Is that a gun in your pocket, or are you just—"

I tug her hair affectionately. Shit, I love this girl.

Maybe if she knows how much she means to me, she'll forgive me for what I'm doing.

The bakery is teaming with customers by the time we get there, and I'm grateful we could be here for Diana. I wouldn't want Beatrice navigating these crowds alone. Jesus. How hard can this be? Chocolate, or vanilla?

An hour later, Diana's narrowed it down to seven different options, and my mind is literally jumbled with words like *fondant* and *buttercream*. The only one that really gets my attention is when the saleslady calls a cake "naked." The girls snort at my reaction until the saleslady

127

explains it means a cake with scant frosting on it that still reveals swaths of plain cake beneath.

"What the hell use is a cake without frosting?" I ask, genuinely confused, which for some reason makes them both giggle harder. I'm losing patience and need to get out of here. I pick up my phone and text Tobias.

You so fucking owe me for this. My balls are shrinking just from sitting in this little pink chair, douchebag.

But before he responds a call comes in. I recognize Patel's number, and I hold up a finger to the girls, walking to the door of the shop. My eyes automatically scan, making sure all's in place, no one suspicious sitting in cars idling outside, nothing out of the ordinary. I can't help it. It's as natural to me as breathing.

"Yeah?" I answer.

"Dude, the only prints we found were yours and your girl's. Sorry, man. Whoever it was had to of worn gloves." Of course they did. I swear softly to myself. "Gotta say there were quite a few of your girl's on the backseat, though," he says with a chuckle. "Wonder how they got there?"

"Fuck you," I say, and he laughs.

"Man in place?"

"He's outside the bakery now, ready to tail her when you come in. Will let you know the second anything surfaces."

"Appreciated, man." I hang up the phone and go back in the shop. I'm not going to think about the fact that I've got someone essentially spying on her. That's not *why* I'm doing it. I've got a helluva lot more to worry about than that.

When I reenter the shop, Beatrice is on her phone and weirdly, she looks guilty. She shoots a furtive look at me, whispers into the phone, then shuts it off and shoves it in her pocket. What the hell? I wait until she joins us and take her by the hand. "Hey, you girls decided yet?"

"Vanilla buttercream with raspberry filling and dark chocolate ganache," Diana says triumphantly.

"Sounds delicious." Thank God. Now we can get out of here. I turn to Beatrice. "Who were you talking to on the phone?"

She looks away. "Just had to answer a question from my bank. Guess they're doing standard checking in on stuff. I, um, maybe spent a lot on the Coach website?" I raise a brow.

"Oh?"

She gives me a sheepish grin. "And I just had to confirm that yes, it was me, and not a theft."

"Baby, how much did you *spend?*"

She looks sheepish. "Just a few…" her voice trails off… "hundred. You know," she shrugs. "I saw a few things I liked and decided it was time for a little splurge." It's her money, and I don't really care as long as she's being responsible, but still, there's something unsettling in the way she's talking.

"Alright then. I gotta hit the office. You and Diana are heading to Verge, right?"

She nods. I'm supposed to meet them all there in a little while. I wouldn't let her go without a man on her, but she's fine now that she's under protection. "I'll drop you off and meet you in an hour."

Diana stands and signs some paperwork, and the three of us leave the cake shop. It's then that I see him. The obscure black Mazda on the corner. For some reason he's vaguely familiar to me, but I can't quite place him. I don't let on that I've seen him, but pull her closer, my hand on the back of her neck. The fucker wants to tail her, he'll have to tail me, and if he's got balls that size it'll be my personal pleasure to meet him head on.

I steer her to my car, open the door, and escort her in. "You sure you don't want me to go with Diana? Save you some time."

"I'm sure, baby." I lean in, barely controlling my temper, ready to fucking kill the person stalking her. I've been at this long enough to know this is no fucking whim of mine. I lean in and buckle her in, lock the door and slam it shut. Her eyes widen, staring at me, but I stalk to my side, pretend to drop something on the ground, and glance at the car. He's got his hand on the wheel, ready to go. I grab my phone, about to dial Patel, when the man catches my eye and pulls away the curb so fast horns blast in protest. The gig's up. He knows I've seen him and now he wants to fucking flee. He heads in my direction and I watch him, but he doesn't stop when he gets to my car, doesn't do anything to Diana, just guns it.

I open the driver's side door and slide in, shut the door, and peel out into the main road, ignoring the sound of honking horns behind me.

"Zack! What are you doing?"

I don't say anything at first, intent on getting behind that son of a bitch who just burned rubber past my car.

"Zack?"

"Someone stalking you, saw me, took off. *Fuck.*"

I try to pull ahead but a huge delivery truck drops its ramp, and a driver starts pushing down a palette of milk crates. I try to get past him but it's impossible, there's a line of busses to my right and when I look in front of me, I see the last bit of black vanish. *Fuck.*

"Who's stalking me?" she whispers. "God, Zack. *Who?*"

I drive toward Verge and say nothing at first. "No fucking clue," I tell her. "But I'll find out."

I PUSH the door open to Tobias's office.

"Hey, man. Have you seen Beatrice?"

He nods. "Yeah, she and Diana were having a drink on the main floor. Everything alright?" I dropped her off here, knowing she was in safe hands with Tobias, while I made sure my men knew exactly what I needed from them.

"Just haven't heard from her yet."

"How long?" he asks, he brows furrowing.

I give him a sheepish smirk. "Like twelve seconds since I texted, just wondering if you saw her."

He half-smiles. "This shit's eatin' you up, huh?"

I huff out a breath, pull out the chair in front of his desk and spin it around, straddling it. "Yeah. Saw a guy I could swear was stalking her today, but I couldn't catch him when he took off, and I asked the guy *I* have tailing her, and he isn't convinced it's what I thought. Thinks it was a fluke."

Tobias leans back in his chair, his dark eyes focused on me, jaw tight. "You know for sure someone's screwing around with her?"

"No doubt, man."

"And what do you have in place?"

"Phone tapped, she's not allowed to go anywhere without my permission, got a man tailing her."

Tobias raises a brow. "Over an arrangement of flowers sent to her?"

"It was more than that," I say, though I know I'm maybe overreacting. "Someone moved my car from where she parked it."

"I don't wanna be an asshole, but she's kinda... forgetful, isn't she?"

I sit up straighter and feel my gut clench. "Sometimes,

but the girl has her shit together and she *knows* someone moved the car." I fill him in on what else that's happened, and he nods speculatively.

"So this kinda shit normally gets around-the-clock surveillance?"

"Shut up." I'm not joking with him now either, and his brows shoot up. "If someone was doing this shit to Diana, what would you do?"

He exhales. "I know. And I know you wanna keep her safe. But I'm just making sure you're not chasing ghosts is all. That's my job, to watch out for you."

My phone buzzes with a message from Beatrice.

At the bar and waiting for you, sir.

"Beatrice," I mutter to Tobias, before I respond.

Only non-alcoholic until I join you. She knows my rule for her.

Yes, sir. Of course, sir.

"Gonna go meet her," I say, pushing up from my chair.

"See you in a bit."

"Who's DM tonight?" I ask, as I open the door to his office. I trust all of them, but I like knowing who the Dungeon Monitor on duty is. "Brax."

Brax is the resident wiseass but he can be trusted.

I push through the office, eager to get to her. Every second apart makes my pulse race, and maybe it's fucked up and maybe Tobias is right and I'm overreacting. I walk through the main entryway door but hear a scream the second I do. On instinct, I break into a run.

I enter the bar area, only to see a few people near the door blink up at me in surprise. No one else has even moved, no one else alarmed. And then I realize, the scream came from the dungeon. *Shit.* I'm so fucking strung up I flinched at a scream. I'm in a BDSM club. People fucking scream. I take a deep breath and try to pretend like I didn't just run in here like a goddamned idiot.

Then I see her. She's sitting at a table right next to the bar, with Diana. Tonight she's in leather pants and a form-fitting top, midnight black and hugging her gorgeous curves. Her hair is loose about her shoulders, and she smiles when she sees me, waving a little. She's safe. She's fine. *God.* I'm the one that isn't. Why'd I bring her here tonight?

She gets up to come to me and walks quickly. I meet her halfway, picking her up in a hug so tight I lift her straight up off the floor. She squeals. "Oh, my. I missed you, too, sir. But it's only been a little while." I put her back on her feet and she tips her head to the side. "Are you okay? You look as if you've just seen a ghost."

"Fine, baby," I say, taking her by the hand and leading he to the bar. "Long day. I need a drink."

Travis fist bumps me, grabs a pint glass, and fills it with frothy beer. He pushes it over. "How's it goin', man?"

"It's going," I say, taking a long pull from the drink.

He gives a little nod toward Beatrice, but his eyes come to me, asking me for permission to get her a drink. "She may," I say. "What's your drink tonight, doll?"

She smiles at me, her blue eyes as lovely as the sky at dusk, bright and hopeful. "Rum and coke, please. Thank you, sir.'

"On my tab, Travis."

"Always," he says.

"For someone with such sadistic tastes, you're quite the old-fashioned gentleman at times," she teases.

I take her drink from Travis, use the straw to extract and take an ice cube in my hand, take her by the wrist, and tug her over to me. Cupping the ice in my hand, I run it along her neck. She gasps, then shivers, as the ice cube melts.

"It's practically evaporating, you're so hot," I tease. She snorts but she braces herself. This isn't easy for her, and I know it. She closes her eyes, allowing me to torture her with the ice, slipping into the submissive headspace I require of her when she's here. I take away the ice cube and place it on a napkin at the bar, then take her collar out of my pocket, sliding it into place. Her eyes flutter open and she bites her lip.

"You ready to play in the dungeon tonight, babe?"

She nods her head eagerly. "Please, sir," she says, her eyes soft and demure. When we're here, she casts off what holds her back, and she's easy for me to read, easy for me to please. She needs to scene to let it all go. And it's one of the very many reasons I love her. It's what I need from her, too.

I take another sip of my beer, then lean in, and whisper to her, "Have you been a good girl today?"

To my surprise her eyes flicker and she looks away. She's hiding something from me, but she casts her eyes down. "No, sir," she says coyly. "I think I need to be punished. *Hard.*"

I tug her hair back to get her attention. Her eyes widen, and her lips form an "o" of surprise. "Sir?" she whispers, teasing gone.

"What did you do?" I ask, taking another sip of my drink. In the corner of the room, laughter breaks out, loud and raucous, and behind me I hear someone purring like a kitten. "Beatrice," I say warningly.

She doesn't answer at first and merely shrugs.

I stand up from the bar, take her by the hand, and lead her to the dungeon. She's either playing this up to be punished, or I need to extract the real truth from her.

Brax catches me at the door and gives me a chin lift. His arms are crossed on his chest as he surveys the room. "Fucking pet store in here tonight," he mutters under his breath. He doesn't judge, but teases mercilessly, so I know it's all in jest. I smile at him, looking around at the dungeon. He's got a point. I've never seen so many tails and collars in my life.

"Someone put an ad out in the paper?" I ask with a snicker.

He chuckles. "Not sure if it's coincidence or what."

"Everyone behaving?" I ask, my tone more serious.

"Yep," he says with a wave of his hand. "All good." He smirks as a dom, a young, college-aged guy who looks like he could be a linebacker, straps his sub to the St. Andrew's cross. "Let the beatings commence." The man rears back with his whip and lets the lash fly.

Beatrice's eyes widen, but then she looks to me and draws a little closer. "Never had a kitten fetish, sir, but I can lick things up with my tongue with the best of them."

My dick twitches in my pants and I want her on her knees. Fuck, I need to relax. I can feel the tension along my shoulders and coiled in my belly. "Tonight, we watch for a while," I tell her, and she barely contains her audible whine. I have a reason, though, and it isn't just for surveillance.

I find an empty leather bench in the corner of the room, sit down, snap my fingers and point for her to take her place kneeling beside me. She drops to her knees, her eyes eager and expectant. I take her chin in my hand and make her look me in the eyes. "Tell me the truth, now. Did you or did you not do something that deserves punishment?"

Her eyes flit quickly away then come back to me. "If I tell you no, will I still be punished?"

I lean in, my fingers still grasping her chin. "I know you want to be punished. What I need to know is if you really deserve it."

She bites her lip and looks away. "I may have, um, forgotten to pay another bill," she says, but she's not looking at me. I frown as she looks back to me. "Sir, are you going to spank me?"

"No." My tone is curter than I intend, her eyes widening. "Not yet. Touch yourself."

She blinks. "Sir?"

"Slide your fingers between your legs," I instruct. "And *touch yourself.*"

Biting her lip, her cheeks a faint tinge of pink, she does what I say, sliding her hand under the edge of her pants.

"Are you wet?" I whisper.

She whimpers a little and nods. "Yes, sir. I am." Her breath hitches, "So wet."

"Were you a bad girl?" I ask her. She bites her lips, her pupils dilating as she strokes herself. Pulling one side of her against my leg, I slap the side of her clothed breast with the palm of my hand. Her eyes go wide, and her mouth drops open.

"Work that clit," I growl, "or you take off that top and I'll punish your bare breasts in front of everyone."

Moaning, grinding against her hand, she whimpers but says nothing to me as I continue to interrogate her.

"Tell me what you did," I say.

"I accidentally stole a bag of chocolate," she gasps, "the little mini ones with the peanuts."

I bite my lip to keep from grinning. My feisty little girl is so damn sweet. I adjust her so she's against my other side and I slap her breast again. "A bag of chocolate? How does someone *accidentally* steal?" Her hand freezes and I squeeze her breast, hard, eliciting a sharp, strangled cry, but then she moans as she finds her clit again, her hand working faster, harder.

"It was under my coat in the cart," she groans. God, she's killing me, talking about chocolate while she's working herself to orgasm. Only Beatrice.

"Naughty girl," I say, then my voice drops, a harsh command. "*Stop.*"

She mewls but obeys.

"Give me your hands," I command.

With a soft whisper of a cry, she does, her beautiful, graceful fingers laying delicately in mine. I lift the fingers that worked her pussy and slide them in my mouth, suckling her sweet juices. She shudders but her eyes stay focused on mine as I lick every drop. Leaning in, I whisper in her ear. "Now grind against my leg." She moves immediately to obey, her legs straddling mine. She writhes against me. I could make her strip. There are others in this room right here, right now, who have hardly a stitch of clothing on. And though sexual play's allowed in the dungeon, most of the sex at Verge takes place behind closed doors. I'm only here to give her what she wants, flirtation with exhibition.

Her orgasms belong to me, and me alone. *I* claim them. But sometimes, I like to make her wait.

I pull her to standing. Without a word, I drag her to the nearest spanking horse, one displayed in the room in front of everyone. I might compromise on giving her what she wants, but I won't strip her. That's only for me, behind closed doors. The bench would push her ass into the air for me to paddle. The horse, however, is more in line with my purposes tonight. With a sturdy, V-shaped structure clad in leather with a padded center strip at the very top, when I push her over it, her breasts will hang on either side, her ass ready for me to punish, and the V-shape will press against her pussy.

What to spank her with?

She hasn't had my belt in a good, long while.

We reach the spanking horse, and I push her gently down over it, allowing my hands to grasp her wrists more firmly than usual. I fasten her wrists at the bottom of the horse. She supports herself by pushing her feet down so she's on her tiptoes on either side of the horse. By now, she'll be fucking soaked.

"You've been a bad, girl, Beatrice," I say. When I take her back to our private room, I want her so ready to come. "Push your pussy against the horse."

Her back arches and she obeys, as I slowly unbuckle my belt, yank it through the loops on my jeans, and double it over, holding the buckle in my fist. We've gotten the attention of several people around us, now, which I know means she's hotter than ever. Still, my mind's on the fucker who's stalking my girl, so the surge of anger I feel at the thought of her stalker makes the first lick of my belt on her ass harder than I intend. The *whap* of leather sounds in my ears, my cock stirring to life, a throb of arousal pulsing low in my belly. I have to calm myself down. Shit, I can't hurt her because I'm angry.

"More," she whispers, her eyes shut tight as her head tips to the side.

I rear back and whip her again with my belt. "Who decides how spankings go?" Three rapid licks of my belt land in succession.

"You do, sir!"

Another wicked stripe lands. If she were naked, she'd welt, but she has the protection of her thin clothing. She'll still feel it, though, and when I peel her clothes off later, I want to see her ass cherry-red, bearing the marks of our session.

"Do I allow you to top from the bottom?" I clip. She shakes her head from side to side. I whip her again, my voice hoarse and tight when I order, "Answer me."

"No, sir," she whispers, grinding her pussy on the horse. "*No, sir.* I'm sorry!"

The whipping begins in earnest then, as I lay stripe after stripe of the folded leather across her upper thighs and ass. She flinches with every lick of the belt, and when a particularly hard one lands at the crease of her thighs and ass, she screams with pain. My cock strains painfully against my jeans, and I whip her harder.

She moans now, with a garbled, "Sir!"

Walking over to her, I place a hand on her lower back and lean in to speak to her. "Are you close, Beatrice?"

"So fucking close," she breathes. "I'm gonna come, Zack. Do you want me to come here? Like this?"

Fuck no. I approve of her warning me with a gentle stroke of my hand along the length of her hair. "Good girl warning me."

"I can't... I can't..." she pants, "Hold onnnn. *Sir.*" It's a plea. I thread my belt quickly back through the loops on my pants and unfasten the straps where her hands are secured.

"You stand right here," I whisper, as I quickly wipe down the bench, house protocol even though she was clothed. I take her by the arm and march her to the indigo room, I barely make it from wanting her so much. I slam the door, push her against it, capture her wrists and pin them above her head while I lean in and claim her with my mouth. I swallow her low hum of approval, then release her hands and slide one hand down between her legs. She slumps against me when I touch her, her eyes closed, head thrown back in bliss. One, two, three swipes of my finger and she's arching.

"May I?" she gasps, remembering our rule to ask before coming by a hair.

"Come, doll. Let it go." I work my fingers faster, firmer, sliding through her slick folds, and then she arches even harder, a strangled cry wringing from her as she writhes in ecstasy. I slide her to the floor, still working her pussy, wrenching the pleasure from her with greed, needing every spasm and thrill as mine. Her climaxes are *mine.* They belong to me, and when I take what's mine I leave nothing behind.

She slumps against me and still I work her, easing her down from her high with gentler strokes. Fuck, I need to be in her. I need to claim her, fill her, let her ride me.

"Sir," she moans on a whisper, her head tipped to the side as if she's high out of her mind, and I know she is, high on arousal and endorphins. The indigo room is meticulously clean and adorned with throw rugs. I chose this one for Beatrice's penchant for subjugation because the floor is warm, and comfortable, as I lay her down on it.

"Take me," she pants. "I need you to fill me. I need you *in* me."

I push up her top and pinch her nipple. "Beg me."

"Please," she pants. "Sir. Oh, God, please fill me. Take me. *Fuck me.*"

"Strip."

She quickly slides out of her clothes, her movements frenzied, eyes shuttered and lust-filled. When she's bared to me, I lift her easily and flip her onto her belly, anchoring myself with a fistful of her hair. She screams when I give it a sharp tug, and my cock throbs, needing to claim her. Grabbing her hips, I drive into her without preamble, drawing out a deep, low moan from her. She shudders when I thrust, her whole body tensing, holding her breath.

I hold onto her and whisper in her ear. "This is my pussy. My hot little cunt. You're my dirty girl."

"Yes, sir," she moans, bracing herself on her arms and knees as I slam into her, the danger she's been under making me want to claim and mark her any way I can. "No one touches what belongs to me," I groan, just before my own climax takes over. I grunt into her ear, my words a jumbled mess of heat and sex and possessive love.

Fuck. *Love.*

As she settles down to the floor, swallowing huge gulps of air, I hold her in my arms, my body surrounding hers, pulling her close to me. I love this woman. I love everything about her. Will I scare her if I tell her?

"You mean so much to me," I whisper, which sounds like some weak-ass shit, but she needs to know what she is to me. Why I do this. And I can't tell her in a way that'll make her close herself off from me.

"And you to me," she says, turning her head to look at me. We're getting there. Every time I whip her ass or tie her up or ask her to obey me, I ask her to *trust* me, and maybe some would say we're coming at this backasswards. But I don't give a shit what some would say.

Beatrice is mine. And I'll keep her safe no matter what that takes.

Chapter 13

The loud clanging of the alarm bursts through my consciousness like a freight train.

"Oh shaddap you," I groan, reaching out to smack it off, but it slides right off the bedside table, unplugs from the charger, and clatters to the floor.

"Shit!" I sit up in bed, my heart smacking against my rib cage. Did I shatter it? I half-fall out of the bed in a move that would rival an Olympic gymnast, twisting my body and reaching the tips of my fingers to grab my phone with my lower body still anchored on the bed. "Don't be broken, don't be broken, don't be broken," I chant, flipping it over, and when I see it's still perfectly fine, I pull myself back into bed and toss the phone back on the table.

Without warning, I feel Zack's colossal palm crack against my naked ass.

"Ow! Hey, wait. I thought you were asleep," I say, rolling over to protect my ass against the sheets and possibly retain a shred of dignity, but since he makes me sleep naked, he now has access to my breasts. I yank the covers up, but it's too late, he's already palming my breasts. He tweaks a nipple, making me shriek.

"Asleep?" He says in a groggy rasp, one eye closed and one half-open, peering at me. He's on his belly, pillow tucked under his chin, utterly and beautifully naked, and I smile in appreciation of the view. "Babe, a drugged man couldn't sleep through that racket. What did your phone ever do to deserve such abuse?"

I sidle over to him and gently nudge him. He rolls over on his back, eyes closed, and pulls me onto his chest. My skin flush against his, I feel the warmth of his body, and his heartbeat thumps against my cheek. I close my eyes and sigh.

"You're purring like a kitten," he chuckles, combing his fingers through my hair. He's right, I am. Half asleep, curled up to him, one knee hitched up over his legs, who wouldn't purr?

"I'll be your kitten. You're into that kinda kink?"

A corner of his lips quirks up. "You need to ask that? Didn't I already make it clear this pussy's mine?"

His hand comes to my neck and he tugs on the collar he left there last night even as I groan out loud. "You did, sir."

Wait… why am I still wearing this collar? I'm not a collared sub, and something inside me fights against this. This is what *Diana* wants, and has for a while. She wears Tobias's collar, and has things like… *rules*. And I know other people at Verge who are into the 24/7 thing where the dom calls the shots and the submissive does what she's told. It's hot, there's no doubt about that. I mean shit, I'm getting wet just laying up on his chest, my ass still stinging from the smack he gave me, my breasts still tingling from the abuse I suffered last night. Just the memory of it makes my pussy throb and zing with need.

But that 24/7 thing isn't *me*.

"Zack, why do I still have this collar on me?" I ask, and even though it feels *so damn nice* to be snuggled up against him like this, I push away from him. I'm not into this. I feel my lips turn down in a frown. "Take it off, please."

He eyes me curiously, his gaze stern as he tugs on my hair. "Watch your attitude."

I blink. "Excuse me? I'm not giving you an attitude." I push away from him, giving him total attitude. "Take this collar off."

His brows rise, his voice stern when he corrects me. "There are other ways of getting what you need without being a brat, young lady."

My heart thumps in my chest, but I ignore it. I've been trained to be turned on by his dominance, that's what this is. He bosses me around and I'm ready to fuck him senseless but *whatever*, this is a simple case of mind over matter.

"We're not at the club," I snap, reaching for my neck. Maybe I can take it off myself. But taking off a collar yourself is like trying to scratch your own back. You can *almost* do it, but the reality is, you need another set of hands. Still, I tug at it, trying to unfasten the buckle, but before I know what's happening, he's up, I'm flat on my back, my wrists are pinned to my sides, and he's over me.

Aw, hell, that's hot. No fair.

"Let me go," I say through gritted teeth. "I didn't do anything wrong."

His eyes narrow, his brows drawing together, deep brown pools that simmer under his finely-honed control. "You're throwing sass at me like confetti at a goddamn wedding, and all I did was forget to take your collar off when you went to bed."

"Weddings? *Jesus.* You have to bring up weddings now? All of this shit kicked off after a wedding, and now I have to see my best friend go through with the whole thing, and do what everyone thinks she should and wear the stupid white dress and get a stupid ring, when all that shit doesn't even *mean* anything when over half the population is going to call it quits anyway so what's even the fucking point?"

He blinks, his grip still tight, but there's surprise in his voice when he speaks. "Christ, Beatrice. What's gotten into you? You PMSing or something?"

I shove him so hard I actually almost budge him. He did *not* just say that. He did *not!* Oh my *gawd.*

"I cannot even believe you just said that," I whisper. "Only total *dickheads* say shit like that."

At that, his whole body tightens, and I just realized I've stepped into total punishment territory for talking to my dom like that. I'm pissed but even I know I probably deserve to be punished. Tobias would whip Diana's ass for mouthing off to him. None of the doms at Verge would put up with this. Even sweet Travis, the bartender, would toss a chick over his knee. There are a lot of hard limits and things like that in this world, but there's one kinda constant: Doms don't do mouthy.

What am I doing? *Who am I?*

He swallows, and I know then he's controlling himself so he doesn't lose his temper. Watching his nostrils flare, feeling the heat radiating from him, I feel sorry for mouthing off over something so small, because it's taking him considerable effort to keep himself in check. He's like a hundred pounds heavier than I am and about five times stronger, and since he wields the power, it's important he doesn't overdo it. But it's the quiet way he speaks to me that subdues me.

"You're right," he said. "That *is* a total dickhead thing to say. I should know better." He's still pinning me in place, and there's no way I'm out of the woods yet. I swallow as he continues. "I'm just shocked that you flipped like this when we were having what I thought was a nice morning, and I'm wondering why."

Tears prick my eyes. "I don't know," I whisper. "I really don't know."

His lips thin and I can see he's warring with himself. Hell, I need him to be stern with me. It's partly why I love him. I close my eyes briefly as emotion overwhelms me.

I love him.

When did I agree to this?

My eyelids flutter open, and he's looking at me with gentleness, the warm brown eyes trained on me. He misses nothing.

"Keep your eyes on me," he whispers, "and listen."

I nod. I mean, I'm pinned beneath this behemoth of a man. What else am I going to do? I decide to play my cards right. "Yes, sir?"

"You don't talk to me that way, Beatrice. I won't allow it."

I nod, still swallowing hard against tears. "Yes, sir." God, it feels so fucking good to call him *sir*. I feel little, and precious, and cared for and I can't deny it's *hot*. It's so wrong but that's partly why I love it.

He works his jaw, his eyes still on me. When he speaks, his voice is both stern and amused. "I can't decide if I should fuck the brat right out of you or punish your ass." He shakes his head from side to side.

"Both?" I suggest on a whisper.

A corner of his mouth quirks up. "Wears me out, keeping up with you."

"I'm a bit of a handful," I say ruefully, suddenly feeling like a total brat.

He releases my wrists, sighs, and gets out of bed. "I'm going to make some coffee." He turns and points a finger at me. "You're staying right there. You have some thinking to do, Beatrice."

"Okay?" Damnit. Is he going to make me think about why I submit to him? Am I going to have to answer questions about what I want from this? I feel like a naughty girl who's been sent to bed.

He turns and looks at me, crossing his arms on his chest. His eyes are stern and probing, the muscles on his shoulders and biceps bulging as he gives me a stern look. "I want you to imagine that I'm going to punish you. When I come back in the room, I'm going to put you over my knee, and spank you for mouthing off. And then we'll talk about how you feel about that."

What?

And then he's gone. I can hardly form a thought as I listen to him in the kitchen, clinking things around and making coffee. Within minutes, the fragrant smell of fresh-made coffee wafts through the air. I realize a few minutes have passed and he's coming back expecting an answer, and all I've done is fantasize about lattes and cappuccino.

Okay, so… he's coming in the room and he's going to spank me. Got it.

A throb of heat pulses low in my belly.

He's going to shut the door, his face all stern and sexy-angry, and then he's sitting on the edge of the bed waiting for me to come to him.

My breathing becomes labored, my pulse quickening.

"What happens to little girls who don't do as they're told?" he'll ask.

I close my eyes and slide my hand under the covers, gliding through my folds. Oh yeah. I'm horny as hell.

I stand in front of him, knowing I'm going to be punished, embarrassed but sort of craving this. Needing him to forgive me for whatever I did. I need to know it's all right now.

I work my clit, and after the sixth stroke of my finger, I

freeze.

Wait. Wait a minute. He didn't ask me to fantasize about getting spanked. That's, like, always gonna turn me on. I frown.

He asked me how I would feel knowing I'd be punished.

I guess… ashamed and yet weirdly, inexplicably… aroused?

Part of me gets angry at him, though. I mean, I'm a grown woman who can take care of herself. Does he think that I can't handle adulting and he needs to treat me like a child? Does he think I'm incapable of taking care of myself? Hell *no*. That's so not cool. I spent my childhood being told I couldn't take care of myself or accept responsibility. I had money handed to me in fistfuls, and to some that sounds like heaven. But when you're twenty years old and legit don't even know how to do a load of laundry and the idea of bank statements is like learning a foreign language, and you've gotten fired from your literal entry-level job that your *daddy* got you because you missed four shifts in a row, it's really not so cool. When you're not good enough at home, and not good enough in the real world, it takes a toll.

And handing control over to a man doesn't solve any of that shit. It doesn't make me more responsible, or stronger, but *dependent* on him and hell no, that isn't happening.

The door swings open and Zack comes in with a tray. He has trays? On the tray are two cups of coffee and a little plate of mini scones, along with a fresh bowl of fruit.

"Wow. Dude. Seriously? I mouth off to you and you bring me breakfast in bed? Is this some sorta alternative reality?"

He raises a brow and smirks, crossing the room to me.

He slides the tray on the bedside table, and lifts the cup of coffee, handing it to me. I take a long sip of piping hot liquid, feeling it course down my throat and warm me through, and sigh.

"Yeah, no," he says. "I wouldn't recommend mouthing off in the future."

I don't know what to say so I reach for a scone, but he taps my hand. "Nope."

I blink up at him.

"I'll feed you." He picks up a scone and it takes everything I have not to smack it out of his bossy hand. Not ten seconds ago I decided I was not that girl who would submit to *real discipline,* and here I am waiting to be fed. I look up to him, and feel the anger rising, my hands shaking with it.

"Tell me what you were thinking," he says, breaking off a piece of scone.

I take a deep breath and let it out slowly before I respond. "I… fantasized about you punishing me and I almost made myself come."

He blinks, then he lifts the piece of scone to my mouth. I let him place it in my mouth, but I'm filled with the sudden desire to *bite* him. He feeds me the piece, and I don't even taste it. I swallow it with a drink of coffee, watching the humor leave his eyes.

"Did you." It isn't a question, but a statement, as if he can't believe what I just told him.

"Yes," I say, growing ornerier by the minute. "And I decided that no. No, I *don't* like the idea of you disciplining me. I like the club scenes and it's hot then, but I worked too hard to get to where I am." My voice is rising, and I push myself up in the bed.

"I see." He places the scone on the plate. "You don't like being accountable to me? You don't like rules and things like that?"

"I... no." My voice comes out tremulously. "Take the collar off, please. And I would like a scone. I don't want to be fed like an animal." I swallow and don't understand why tears spring to my eyes as I speak. "I like playing with you at the club. I like scening. But I don't want anything beyond that, Zack."

He places a scone on a plate and hands it to me. "I see," he repeats.

Does he?

He gets to his feet. "I'm going to take a shower. Eat your breakfast. After breakfast, we'll talk about what you have going on today, and plan when you'll check in with me."

What did I expect? An argument? Well yeah. Maybe I did. Why, if he's giving me exactly what I want, do I feel so sad?

"Okay," I say, taking a quick bite of scone and washing it down with coffee to swallow over the lump in my throat. I want to say *yes, sir.* But no.

No.

"I'm not sure we need to check in?" I ask, though my voice is curt. "I mean, the reality is, I'm good. You know? If anyone tries to hurt me, I'll pepper spray them." I polish off the scone, finish my coffee, and push myself out of bed.

He eyes me thoughtfully, stroking his chin, nodding. "Right."

Why is he so calm about this? My head is going to explode, and my heart feels like it's shattering. I want to whip my plate across the room and watch it fracture into a million pointy shards.

I've taken a whipping from this man. I've been tied up and fucked senseless, gagged and degraded, and in some distant past, that was hot. That, I could take. Then why do I feel like the calm acceptance of what I'm telling him might break me? He crosses his arms and looks at me thoughtfully. "We'll have rules at Verge," he says, the barest trace of sarcasm in his tone. "Unless you want to stop that, too?"

"No! I mean... I don't think so," I say.

"Just so we're clear, when we're at the club, you're submissive to me. Yes?"

"Well, yeah."

"Yeah. Ok. I'm gonna shower. Finish breakfast, and then we'll get going." He pauses, his jaw clenches and he opens his mouth as if to say something, then shakes his head and leaves.

What the hell has come over me?

I'm thankful the shower running drowns out the sound of my crying.

I pick up the phone and text Diana.

We need to talk.

Babe, you ok?

I think so. Can you talk?

Of course. At Verge?

I exhale. *Somewhere else?*

Books and Cups?

A club member, Marla, has a bookstore with a coffee shop close to Verge.

Yes. Perfect.

Do you need to ask Zack first?

I pause, take a deep breath, clench my teeth and then reply.

No.

━━

I PAY the Uber driver and walk with purpose to the coffee shop where Diana's waiting for me when my phone buzzes.

I look at the screen, not surprised it's Zack, though I half-expected him to call me earlier than this. After I showered, I told him I was going to meet her. He frowned but nodded, then he let me go. I actually caught myself looking over my shoulder for him, wondering if he'd follow me. It was unusual for him to allow me to go without any argument.

Frowning, I ignore the little voice in my head that tells me to stop acting like a baby. I'm doing the *opposite*, actually. I need to do this for me. To prove that I can.

When I reach the bookstore, I push open the door and smile at Marla. "Hey, Beatrice," she calls out from behind the counter. I wave, and she looks behind me as if expecting to see someone else.

For Christ's sake. It takes me a minute to realize she's looking for Zack.

"No Zack today?" she asks curiously.

I shake my head and grit my teeth. "No, not today."

"I'm just surprised. He's been following you everywhere you go, watching you so closely after those things happened. It's weird seeing you alone. I just—"

"I'm fine," I say with a forced smile.

"Right," comes a voice behind me. I look over my shoulder to see Diana standing behind me with a friendly smile for Marla, but knowledge in her eyes. She knows I'm bluffing. I am *so not fine*. Why the hell did I agree to coffee? I need something a helluva lot stronger than that.

"You girls going to the club tonight?" Marla asks, as she fills our coffee orders.

I shrug. "I don't know. I have to see if Zack is free. I think I'd like to, but I'm not sure."

"I'm on my way there in a little bit," Diana says, taking her mug from Marla. "I'm doing some paperwork with Tobias before we open later."

I like that she says *we*, and grin to myself. We carry our mugs over to a small, circular table in the back of the store, and slide into chairs. "Who knew my best friend would become part owner of a BDSM club?" I say with a laugh. "Happy wedding, babe. Here's some engraved nipple clamps."

She snorts. "Who'd have thought the most independent woman I know would be found crawling *on her knees* to a Dom and getting her ass spanked in public?" She takes a sip of coffee and wiggles her eyebrows at me.

"You heard about that?"

She snorts. "Uh, *yeah.*"

Jesus.

"Why don't you say that a little louder," I snap, putting the mug up to my lips and taking a sip so I have an excuse not to talk.

Diana blinks up at me in surprise, her brows raising, before she nods slowly. "Spill, Bea."

I shrug. Now that I'm here, I'm not quite sure I actually want to tell her anything. But I reached out to her for a reason, and we don't hold shit back from each other.

"I told Zack I don't want rules anymore." Now that I've said it, it doesn't sound so bad.

She whistles and puts her mug back down. *"Reallly."*

I wave off a hand. "It's a not a big deal. Listen, different people like different things. You know? There is *nothing wrong* with wanting to *just* scene. For wanting not to... you know. Do other things. I mean, seriously, *most* people just want to scene."

"Right. Of course," she agrees, leaning back and folding her hands in her lap. I look at her large, hazel eyes, and my nose tingles. There's nothing but compassion in her eyes, but she knows me so well, it hurts to be sitting in front of her split open like this. "I'd never judge a dynamic or relationship. There are *lots* of people who just want to scene, and there's nothing wrong with that. Just like there are lots of people who don't even want to scene. You know. People like vanilla, too."

I hear a gagging noise and look up to see Marla's face twisted at us as she puts a box of books on the ground near us. "Vanilla," she huffs. "Utterly tasteless." But she winks and walks away, giving us space.

"And just because someone wants to scene and doesn't want a 24/7 dynamic... I mean hell, girl, I help run a BDSM Club. I know *all kinds* of walks of life and I do not judge. But *you're* not most people."

I take another sip of coffee and wish it was hotter than this. Weirdly, I want it to hurt, scald me when I drink it. I won't look at her, but I listen, even though her words cut me because I think she may be onto something.

"*You* need more than scening, Bea. You're happiest when Zack is *totally* in control. We've talked about this. You love when he holds you accountable. You know this."

Do I?

"Maybe I've outgrown it," I say with a shrug. Her eyes go dark at that and she purses her lips. "Listen," I say, trying to dig myself out of this hole, "I'm not talking about *you*, okay? So don't take it that way. I'm talking about me."

Her expression doesn't change as she takes a sip of coffee.

"What?" I ask, sipping my own coffee to quell my anger. I want to smack her. I love her, but she has the most annoying habit of always being right.

Grrr.

"You know what," she says, her eyes twinkling like stars at dusk, hinting at humor but warning of impending nightfall. "Sure, people outgrow things. But I know you too well.

I know that you're just using that as an excuse to deflect the real reason."

"Shut up." Her eyes shutter at the barb in my voice and she calmly places her mug down and folds her hand in her lap. Diana used to have a temper that matched mine, but as Tobias' long-term sub, she's learned to calm herself down, and her implacable face makes me even angrier. "Stop judging me."

"I'm not judging you."

I feel like a bitch for snapping at my best friend, but I can't stop the waves of emotion that are crashing inside me. I want to cry and scream and rip things apart. I say nothing because I don't trust myself to talk. If I open my mouth, I'll lose my shit. And I'm trying to be the person that *doesn't lose her shit*, so spilling my guts now would sorta be counterintuitive.

"I'm just stating facts, babe," Diana says. She shakes her head and her eyes gentle as she leans on the table on her elbows, leaning into me. "You're the one who made me go to Tobias when we were in a rocky place and I didn't believe that it was worth fighting for. You were the one who helped me see that it *was* worth fighting for. And because I love you, I need to do this for you now, to help you see beyond your own... your own..."

"Stupidity?" I snap, my temper barely in check.

"No, Bea," she says softly. "Stubbornness. Honey, this isn't about stupid or smart or anything like that." Her voice lowers, teeming with emotion when she speaks, so softly I can barely hear her. "This is about fear. It's about facing our fears. I was afraid to go back to Tobias and make this work because I was afraid he'd reject me like all the other losers I'd dated, and it was fear that made me say *oh hell no.*"

The lump dissolves in my throat and I don't even

realize I'm crying until Diana reaches in her bag and hands me a tissue. But like the good friend that she is, she doesn't stop talking but pushes through, telling me what I need to hear. "That's the beauty of submission, Beatrice. It's why the relationships that work are stronger *faster*. The connection is deeper. You face the fears that everyone faces, but it's amped up to ten, and when you face the fear with someone you trust, you draw closer."

Aw, fuck my life. Honest to God, why do the people I love most always have to be right?

I don't say anything but swipe at my tears, unable to stop the vision of me on my knees at Verge in front of Zack. He's holding a pair of metal clamps in his hand, and I'm shaking with anticipation. I know it's going to hurt. But it's standing on the precipice of fear before he reels me back into him that makes it so damn hot. It's facing fear and pain but trusting him not to take it too far. I blink back tears as Diana presses on.

"That's what love is, Beatrice. Every day I put my son on that bus and trust that he's in good hands, and a little part of me dies every time. Knowing that he's under someone else's care and not mine and trusting that they'll take good care of him. This is what love is about." Her voice teems with emotion as she continues. "We don't know what will happen from one minute to the next but hell, we're *doing it anyway*. It could break us." She reaches for my hand and squeezes. "And sometimes, it does. But sometimes? We need to be broken so we can be put back together again."

I wipe away the tears that keep flowing. "God, I love you, you bitch," I mutter, which makes her laugh out loud and toss a wadded-up napkin at me.

"Jesus, I think I need to start serving alcohol in here," Marla says. "Irish cream in your coffee, ladies?" She's standing far enough she hasn't heard what we've said, but close enough that she can see us both wiping at our eyes.

"Tobias would spank her pert little ass," I say, needing to get back on firm footing.

"And Zack would spank *your* pert little ass," Diana says.

Marla's gaze grows wistful, but she simply smiles. "Lucky girls," she says with feeling, before she turns and walks away.

Lucky girl.

Am I?

"Babe, I gotta go," Diana says, looking at her phone. "I told Tobias I'd meet him in fifteen minutes. Walk with me to Verge?"

I nod, and we tidy up our table, say good-bye to Marla, and head to Verge, which is only a few blocks away. It feels weird not telling Zack where I'm going or when, but I'm embracing this now. This is my freedom, what I want and need and I'm not taking it back now. I listened to what Diana said, but I have to let it simmer a bit. It feels weird, like I've been walking on a tightrope with nets below and now I'm going it alone, balancing myself mid-air with no safeties in place.

You want this, I tell myself. *This is what you want.*

I blink in the bright light of an autumn afternoon and notice someone watching me from across the street. At first, I don't really give it much thought. I mean, the streets of New York are crowded with people. But when the man staring at me quickly looks away, then speaks into his phone, something in my belly clenches. This is… weird. Am I beginning to see ghosts like Zack does?

My phone rings and when I look at the number, I see it's Zack.

I silence it and walk with Diana. I'll call him later, when I'm good and ready.

Chapter 14

I've called her twice and she isn't returning my calls. What the actual fuck is going on? I can tell by my tracking app on my phone that she's left the bookstore, then why won't she pick up? This morning, I had no idea where her fit came from, and I'm still not sure what I think about it. I'm a fucking dom.

But is she a sub?

She flourishes under our kink at the club, and it's hot as hell. I love her even when she makes me half-crazy. She doesn't want the serious side of things? Hell, I have to respect that. I can't do anything but *admire* that about her. But where did this come from? Where does this leave us?

I yank open the entryway door to Verge enter the key code. No one's at the door yet since it isn't opened, but Tobias is here, and I need to get my shit together before I see her. I stalk through the main entrance and head to Tobias's office, but before I get there, I hear two familiar voices in the lobby.

"I have no idea, but it's likely in my head. And you

know what? I don't need to tell him every little thing that's going on. If Carter wants to call me, he can call me."

A chill goes down my spine. It's Beatrice talking to Diana.

Who the fuck is Carter?

I come around the corner and the two of them blink up in surprise at me. I nod. "Diana. Beatrice, I didn't expect to see you here. But then again, you didn't tell me where you were going, so I wouldn't know."

She crosses her arms on her chest, and despite the pink that colors her cheeks and the way her eyes flash at me, she's hot as hell. Jesus, she's maybe even sexier all mad like this. I want to fist her hair and draw that head back, make her mouth part open in surprise, and then claim that mouth with mine before I spank her ass for going off the fucking rails like this. The dom in me itches to tame this willful, headstrong girl.

"I came to see Diana. I needed to talk with her. And since she was on her way here to see Tobias, I came with her."

Hands on my hips, I turn to Diana. "Came to see Tobias? Let me ask you something. Did you leave without telling him where you were going? Show up here unannounced?"

Diana's eyes look pained as she glances from me to Beatrice, and when she speaks her voice is gentle. "No, Zack. But Tobias is my long-term Dominant and soon-to-be-husband. We have rules, and I like it that way."

God, I'm a dick for dragging her into this. I know she's right.

"Hey, man," Tobias says from the doorway. "What's going on?"

Beatrice speaks up. "We have an issue we're dealing with, Tobias," she says, effectively asking him to butt out.

Tobias looks with surprise from me to Beatrice. "I see. Well, why don't you two head to the private rooms? No one's coming here for a while, give you some space to sort this out?"

And then I remember what she said this morning.

When we're at Verge, she's mine.

"I think that's an *excellent* idea," I say, crossing the room and taking Beatrice by the hand. She tries to pull away, but I hold fast and slip my hand to her wrist instead, a firmer grip. "You said at Verge, you were my sub," I say low in her ear.

"Yes," she grits out, teeth clenched. "I did, didn't I?"

I look at her and see more than anger in the pretty blue eyes that flash at me like a storming sea. I can't read her look, though, but I feel her tension. On a normal day, a sound spanking would knock down that wall she's holding up between us. But today is not a normal day.

"Will you safeword?" I ask her, challenging her. If we walk through those doors, her ass is mine, and she knows it. Yeah, she could safeword in there, and I'd have to listen, but there's more than a scene going on here. It isn't always smart to scene when you're pissed at your—sub, or whatever she is. Girlfriend? Jesus, some would say fiancée. But we need to talk, and privacy is the answer.

"I'm not safewording, *sir*," she says through clenched teeth. "Unless you think you can't handle me?"

I can't help but chuckle at that. "You want to bait me, doll? How do you think that'll end up for you?"

She doesn't answer, which is frankly answer enough for me. I lead her through the entryway door into the club proper, past the bar, past the demo rooms and dungeon, and straight to the private rooms. Silence descends on us like dark velvet, nearly oppressive, the vacant bar and community areas underscoring that the two of us are *alone*.

I don't even know why she's so pissed at me, but she agreed to submit to me when we're at Verge. Maybe she didn't plan on seeing me today, but I feel like shit's spiraling out of control. She's given me the green light to dom her here so, hell, I'm stupid not to take advantage of that. When we get to the room, I open the door, push her over the threshold, then shut it behind me.

"Strip."

She turns around to face me and opens her mouth. I stand in front of the doorway, arms crossed on my chest, eyes narrowing on her. I watch as she weighs her options. She can do what I say. She can defy me and push me to make her obey, which is sometimes part of the scene here, and I'd be lying if I said I didn't want that. Or she can safeword, and end this.

End what?

Us. Fucking everything. I don't even know how to do this shit without the power exchange. How do I care for a woman who doesn't submit to me? Telling me I can't dom her is like telling me to drive with my eyes closed.

Yeah, no. If this is no for her, then... Jesus. It's a no for *us*.

I watch as she makes the conscious decision, her fingers grasping the edge of her white top, jaw clenched. Her hands freeze, and her eyes meet mine. "And if I tell you no?"

"Tell me no, or safeword?"

She swallows. To some this is a game, but hell, nothing's ever been so real between us.

"I'm not *fucking* safewording," she says, her voice cracking as tears dampen her eyes, and at that I've had it.

She may not know what she needs but hell, I do.

"And you're not fucking defying me." The game ends now.

I reach for the buckle of my belt and unfasten it, my eyes on her. She swallows and stands her ground, not moving, but when I yank it through the loops of my pants, she flinches. Beatrice has been on the receiving end of a caning, a lexan paddle, and a stout whip. She can take pain. She doesn't flinch because of the knowledge her ass is about to be whipped. There's more to this and hell, I'm drawing this out like poison from a wound.

For a strapping I'd normally have her bend over the bed or a spanking bench, but I know she's in no mood to do what she's told.

Doubling the belt over in my hand and holding the buckle, I step over to where she stands and take her by the arm.

"Ow," she says. It's almost cute how she protests against what we both know she needs.

"Ow? I'm not hurting you." She'll be saying *ow* before I'm done.

She yanks away from me, trying to pull her arm out of my grip but I'm prepared for the fight and tighten the hold I have, stepping up my pace.

"Why are you doing this?" she whines. "God, Zack. I didn't do anything wrong." Yeah, that's what I'd call a last-ditch effort. I sit on the edge of the bed, spin her out, then yank her straight across my lap. I don't even bother to bare her. This isn't about sex. Not yet.

"You said I can dom you at the club, and now we're here."

I press one arm across her lower back, pin her legs against mine, bring the belt back, and lash it against her ass. She screams, louder than I've ever heard her. She's taken a whipping from me and not screamed that loud, so I suspect this has more to do with anger than pain.

Jesus, I can't deny it feels good to whack her rebellious

ass. I give her another hard spank, then another. Her screams raise in pitch and she's fighting me hard, but I'm stronger, and it's easy to master her. I take in a deep, calming breath. If I'm punishing her, I can't lose my control. I see my purpose with utter precision.

"You've thrown up your walls and defied me. You're refusing to communicate with me. And if you don't want this, you tell me now. You *safeword*."

My range of motion with her over my knee is limited, but the belt meets its mark. The rise and fall of my belt is almost methodical, a rhythmic *swish* and *thwap* between her cries and flinching. My erection presses up against her belly, but I press on. I'm not done until she caves. At the sixth smack of the belt, I drop it on the floor. This isn't getting me where I need to be. In one swift move, I shove down her leggings and bare her before I raise my hand and smack my palm against her bare skin. She cries out but it's more subdued this time and ends on a whimper.

With hard, measured strokes of my palm, I know the moment the brat goes right out of her, as she goes from fighting me and screaming to sniffling, wet drops damp-ening my pants. She holds onto my leg but her body slumps over my knee. I pause, running my palm over her scorched ass, hot to the touch, smoothing her beautiful curves. I'm not angry at her anymore. Minutes pass as she cries softly, and I rub out the sting, massaging her punished bottom. I gather her hair and move it off her neck, inhaling the scent of vanilla, before I run my fingers along the soft, satiny skin. Jesus, she's beautiful.

"C'mere," I murmur softly, releasing the grip I have on her lower back, lifting my leg off hers, and turning her around across my lap. I pull her into me, my eyes closing as she burrows into my arms and sobs against my chest. "Baby," I whisper, tucking her into me as tightly as I can hold her. I rock her, holding her so close she has to push her head up for breath, and when she does, her eyes meet mine.

"God, I needed that," she whispers. "I don't know what the hell got into me. I just... suddenly... I was..."

"Shhh."

"You want me not to talk, sir?"

There it is. *Sir.* My arms tighten around her and my chest warms with the simplest gesture of submission.

"Talk all you want, doll. You just don't have to." And isn't that what this is about? I'm offering her a chance to lean on me, to give me her fears and uncertainties, and trust me with her heart.

She relaxes against me as if she's falling asleep, and a soft smile plays on her lips. I bend down and brush my lips against hers.

"Sometimes I think I need to just be reminded of how things can be," she says. But as I hold her, her body suddenly stiffens. "Zack?"

"Yeah, baby?"

"How did you know I was here?"

Dammit. I release a shuddering breath. Beatrice fucked up when she flipped out on me. But I fucked up by hiding from her. I need her to trust me, and I might have screwed that up royally. I can only tell her the truth and hope she knows I love her.

My grip on her tightens. "I was tracking you, baby. Only so I can keep you safe."

Her body goes rigid and her eyes meet mine, widened in disbelief. She pushes herself off my lap and rights herself, pulling up her leggings.

"Define *tracking.*"

I rake a hand through my hair and huff out a breath. "I've had a man on you, making sure you're safe."

Her jaw drops.

Shit. This is not how I wanted to tell her.

"Without telling me?" she whispers.

"I… yeah," I say with a sigh. "I just needed to keep you safe, baby. It has nothing to do with not trusting you or anything."

She gestures to the bed and to the floor where my belt still lies. "You just spanked me to tears," she whispers. "You just… and you…" Her voice trails off. "You want me to trust you, and yet you were fucking *tracking me?*"

I get to my feet, my voice rising with hers. "Beatrice, it isn't like that. *Listen*, baby."

But she shakes her head and holds up her palm. "Don't," she says, her voice cracking, like the snap of branches in winter. "Don't, Zack," she whispers, wiping her eyes. "Please. I'm leaving." She shakes her head, gold tumbling on her shoulders. "Call your men off." She closes her eyes and her head falls back if she's steeling herself for what she says next. "And whatever you do, don't you dare follow me."

She turns on her heel, marches to the door, and slams it with a bang that reverberates within the chambers of my heart.

———

"LUCIANO."

"Yes, sir?"

I'm sitting in the bar area at Verge. I need to connect with man I've had on her. Diana peeked her head in a little while ago, smiling sadly at me, and I can only assume that she saw Beatrice as she left the building. Tobias darkened the doorway briefly, as I was dialing my phone, but when I didn't return his look or speak to him, he left, too. I'm grateful they don't want to talk to me. I'm doing what I can to keep my shit together as I pull the team off Beatrice.

"You're relieved of your duties."

"Sir?"

"There will be no need to monitor Beatrice's safety from now on."

"I see." There's a brief pause, and my gaze wanders about the vacant bar area. Where is she now? Where did she go? What is she feeling?

"Then you don't want to know where she's gone or what she's doing," Luciano says.

My jaw clenches. "No."

"All right," he says in a singsong voice, as if he's taunting me. What the fuck is this?

"Luciano, you have something to tell me, you fucking tell me. Then we hang up this phone and I reassign you." I clench my jaw and stare at the picture frames on the wall, unseeing.

"I'm sorry, sir," he stutters. "It's just that less than a minute ago, she got into the car of a man I'm tracking now." I hear the sound of an engine accelerating.

"Right." I stand, walking without seeing around the bar, my mind teeming with possibilities. The right thing to do would be to let her go, to trust that she's with a friend or someone she knows. She's with a man? Who is he? Is it someone she's known for a while? I pace the floor, torn between asking the obvious and respecting her privacy. "What of it?"

"This is the fourth time he's crossed her path. I don't know who he is, but he's no harmless bystander."

Fuck. I need to know. I recall the guy I saw when we left the cake shop, dark hair and eyes behind shades, vaguely familiar. I stare at the pictures on the wall above the loveseats, my mind racing as if putting the pieces of a puzzle together. It's right here. There's something right at the edge of my memory involving Beatrice and her family.

The knowledge hits me with a flare of recognition like sun breaking through clouds on a summer day, blinding and vivid, the picture frames tipping me off. The man I saw outside the cake shop I'd seen before, but not in person. I'd seen him in a picture frame on the way upstairs from her father's man cave. Her foster brother.

"Luciano, run the background of a foster child who stayed at Beatrice's parents' home, and get back to me as soon as you have any information."

But there's no sound on the other end of the line.

Chapter 15

I fling open the door to Verge and walk into the brisk autumn air while brushing away tears. How could he *do* this? And to reveal this after breaking down my walls like that? I close my eyes and stomp my feet, pretending it's to keep me warm, but I know better.

"Bea?"

A man's voice calls out and shakes me out of my stupor. I blink, looking around me, and see a cab at the curb, the door flung open.

"Carter?" I haven't seen him in so long I barely recognize him. God, he looks like shit. His eyes are bloodshot, and though he wears a hooded sweatshirt, it hangs loose on him, like an elephant skin. Still, he smiles, and the little girl in me who misses him smiles back.

"What are you doing here?"

"I was thinking about you, and driving on my way to lunch," he says, "and there you are." When he smiles at me like that, the grin splits his face in two and makes my heart squeeze.

I wrap my hands around my belly as if to protect

myself but I'm not myself. I don't even know what I think about what's happening with Zack. Just when he's brought me back to where I'm happy, curled up on his lap and holding onto him like he's my life preserver, he dashes cold water on me, reminding me that he's an overprotective bear who's stifling the hell out of me. It's *so not cool* that he had someone fucking *tracking* me without my knowledge. He wants me to trust him but hell, how can I if he doesn't even trust *me?*

I shiver in the brisk fall air as Carter steps out to greet me, embracing me. I think it odd that he does. He was never one for physical affection. It should be nice to see a familiar face at a time like this, when it seems as if my world is crumbling around me, but I fight the desire to turn tail and run. I'm not sure why.

I agree to join him for lunch but when I'm sitting in the back of the cab that smells like stale coffee and cigarettes, I wonder if I did the right thing.

No, I tell myself. *You're just used to telling Zack everything. Just let it go.*

"So good to see you," I say. "And what a nice surprise that you're here. How are you?"

"Fine," he says, but his smile is sad now. He turns to look out the window. "I hear you're engaged."

Shit. How could I have forgotten about that? Everyone in the world thinks I'm marrying Zack, and now I have to not only break up with him, I need to tell the world we're not engaged anymore and we were never fucking engaged to *begin* with.

For *fuck's* sake.

"I'm not engaged," I blurt out, ignoring the way he whips his head around to look at me.

"You're not?" I expect him to blink in surprise, but instead his gaze darkens like sudden storm clouds rolling in on a summer day. He curses under his breath, and I startle to see little flecks of spittle form at the corners of his mouth. What the hell is this?

"No," I whisper. "I just broke up with my—with Zack."

Something is wrong. Something is terribly *wrong*.

My heartbeat races and I look wildly out the window. Where are we going? Waves of nausea swirl in my belly, and I reach for my phone on instinct. I pat the side of my bag where my phone goes, but it's empty. With frantic, rapid movements I rifle through my purse, only to see that my phone is missing.

"You're not engaged," he repeats. Why does the sudden knowledge incite such fury in him?

"No, Carter. Why... what's wrong?" I look wildly about the inside of the cab, looking for my phone, but it's not here. I peer through the screen that separates us from the driver. It's getting dark out, and I have no idea where I am. Neon signs flash past our windows, and still we drive on.

"Call my phone?" I ask him.

"You won't find your phone," he says lazily with a sigh as he looks out the window. "And I'm sorry, Beatrice. I never would've gone through with this if I'd known the engagement was off. *Jesus.*"

I shiver, trying to keep my head clear, even though I'm dizzy and breathing is becoming difficult.

"What are you talking about?" I ask in a whisper, not trusting myself. "What the *hell* are you talking about?"

"She told me you were engaged," he says, his voice tight like bow strings ready to snap.

"Who? Carter, what the *hell?*"

He just shakes his head. I grab at the divider to get the driver's attention, desperation clawing at my chest. "Hey. Hey!" My voice is high-pitched and sounds distant. "Pull the car over. Now! Let me out!" But the driver, an anonymous man wearing a black, rimmed cap and a long-sleeved black t-shirt, doesn't even turn to look at me. "Hey! This is kidnapping! I told you to let me out, so let me the hell *out* of here." The cab moves faster, the engine accelerating so quickly my head snaps back.

Shit.

"Carter, this is illegal. I have no idea what you're doing, but you need to let me the hell out of here."

He shakes his head, his eyes distant and cold. "It's too late for that, Bea. Way too late. Did you know your boyfriend had a tracking device on your phone?" He laughs. "It's why I had to get rid of it outside your little club."

He tilts his head to the side, as the car moves so quickly my stomach churns. "And you're okay with that level of control?" He shakes his head. "She's right. He's so wrong for you. It's too bad you didn't realize that before it was too late."

"*Who?* What the hell are you doing?"

Bile stings the back of my throat and I fight the desire to vomit. How much does he know? Was he aware of the conversation I had this morning with Zack?

Everything around me seems suddenly too vivid, too clear, the stains on the back of the seat in front of me, the worn plush fabric beneath my hands as I push my palms down to steady me, the sound of Carter's breathing.

"I was always nice to you, Carter. I never hurt you. I don't understand why you'd do something to me." I swallow the lump in my throat, memory after memory of the time I spent with him when he was younger flashing in my mind like a movie reel on fast forward. Is this what people mean when they say their life flashed before their eyes? Does this mean I'm going to die?

Why?

I'm not the girl with millions anymore. I know nothing that would make me a target for anyone.

He doesn't answer me.

The light around us vanishes, and we're suddenly plunged into darkness. I close my eyes and breathe in deeply, trying to steady my nerves, before my lids flutter open and I look wildly about me. Talking has done no good, so now it's important I keep my head about me. Irrationally, I expect Zack to come flying around the corner any minute to save me, but the knowledge that he won't makes me choke out a dry sob. He's gone. I pushed him away. The tracker on my phone is useless, and whoever is orchestrating this knows too much. I have to find a way to safety on my own.

The cab pulls to a stop, and I can't see where we are, as it's pitch black wherever we've parked.

"Stay calm, Beatrice," Carter says, then his hand is on my wrist, pinching me so hard it hurts. I pull away, but he only grips harder. My door swings open, and the driver is standing there. He reaches for my other hand, Carter releases me, and I'm yanked out into musky, dank air. I blink, looking up at the driver's face, my breath going out of me as I stare into the familiar lewd grin of Judson Tolstoy Hayes.

Chapter 16

"We can run back reels on her exit and right outside our door, but no more than that, Zack." Diana paces Tobias's office, wringing her hands, while Tobias runs through the security cameras by his desk, and I alert my buddies on the force to get their asses over here and help me get my girl back.

"I knew something was wrong," Diana wails. "She hasn't been herself lately."

I turn to look at her, taking a deep, cleansing breath so I don't snap. I'm angered at her dramatics, even though I know they're justified. I want facts, and *now*.

"Tell me what you know."

Diana blinks up at me, her gaze swiftly meeting Tobias' but Tobias is scrolling through security feed.

"*Diana.*"

Tobias looks over and realizes she's hesitating. "For Christ's sake. Spill, woman," he barks out.

Diana looks pained as she speaks. "She said she wasn't into the whole 24/7 thing and that maybe... maybe she outgrew the dynamic."

I wave an impatient hand in the air. "Yeah, I know that. I mean tell me anything else that was out of the ordinary. Anything at all."

She frowns. "*That* was out of the ordinary."

I anchor my hands on my hips, my mind teeming with possibilities and ideas. She has a point, and it's partly why it's baffled me. Beatrice loves submitting to me, and yeah, I get that she might not want rules and a more serious dynamic, but I wouldn't have pursued this relationship with her if it hadn't been such a good fit. She's feisty as hell, but I love that about her.

"Go on."

"It was after the whole fake engagement thing," she says. "Zack, c'mon, she was different after that, wasn't she?"

Hell yeah she was. I nod, listening, impatient as I'm ready to fucking raze New York City to find Beatrice and I don't have patience to talk about this shit.

"Her parents putting all that pressure on her, and then people congratulating you on your engagement that wasn't really one anyway? And then when her brother called..."

"Her brother," I repeat. My suspicions are confirmed, then. Luciano was tracking someone before his phone went dead. Her brother's the one who was stalking her, and fuck if he isn't the one now who's involved in this.

I whip out my phone and call into my office. I need her parents on the phone, *now*.

Chapter 17

We're in some sort of dark alleyway. Judson has me by the arm, gripping so tightly I can feel my bones rubbing together, and the muscles burning.

"You're hurting me," I hiss. "Let me go. *God,* when Zack finds you, he'll *kill* you. He will *kill* you."

He laughs mirthlessly. "Ah, if I let you go, you'll run or do something stupid. Before I do so, we need to have a talk, you and I, just the two of us. And if we don't, then I may *have* to hurt you." A slow, sinister smile, like a snake coiling, curls his lip upward. "But maybe you'd like that. My men say you like to be hurt. Don't you, Beatrice?"

"Fuck you."

His grip tightens, and I let out an involuntary squeak. Tears blind my eyes, and I look helplessly to Carter, but his eyes are cast down as he marches beside me in silence.

"Open the door," Judson says. I look wildly about us, knowing that if he pulls me into this building that looms in front of us, we're not exactly sitting down for a cup of coffee. The further I get away from civilization, the less of a chance I get for calling for help. My stomach clenches as

I look around me, and his grip becomes so tight I can hardly breathe.

"You say a word to anyone, I'll shoot him dead, Beatrice." Judson flicks the edge of his jacket, revealing the gleam of a silver revolver tucked in the waistband of his pants. He'll shoot Carter? I look quickly to Carter, who doesn't meet my eyes. His jaw is tight, his nostrils flaring. What the hell is going on?

Carter steps in front of us, waves a keycard, and I hear the click of a door unlocking. Carter wrenches it open, the bottom of the door squeaking along the concrete like nails on a chalkboard.

"After you, my lady," Judson says with fake courtesy, and I consider stomping the top of his shiny shoe and kneeing him in the groin. But would he shoot Carter? Would I care?

Hell yes, I would. Even though he betrayed me.

I step inside the doorway, taking in every detail around me. There has to be some way for me to get out of here, some way to notify others. *Some way for Zack to find me.* My mind is a jumble of confused thoughts, though. I mean, not an hour ago I was telling him to leave me the hell alone. I was furious at him for having someone watch me and give me rules, but now, here in the dim light of a flickering street lamp, looking into the sinister eyes of Judson, I want nothing more than Zack's arms around me. This is a hell of a time to be having regrets, but shit, I can't help it.

Maybe I was wrong. I was *so fucking wrong.*

He pulls me into a narrow hallway that smells of sweat and desperation. I walk beside him silently, contemplating my options. If I twist my arm and knee him, I could get his gun, and then...

And then what? I have no phone. I have no way of getting out of here, and no idea what Carter would do even if by some miracle I was able to get away from Judson.

"Why, Carter?" I ask, as Judson leads me to a room that looks like it was once well-kept. There's a dim chandelier overhead, a gleaming table with an assortment of chairs, and books on shelves. It looks like some sort of library. Judson removes his weapon and points at a chair for me to sit in.

"Sit."

"I just want to know *why,*" I say to Carter. "I did nothing to either of you, and out of the blue you kidnap me? What the fuck *is* this?"

"You were marrying a man beneath you," Judson says, laying his gun down on a small table with cold precision. "Years ago, you were betrothed to *me,* Beatrice."

"I was never *betrothed* to you," I sputter. "Are you out of your mind?"

Carter's eyes widen as he looks from me to Judson, confirming what I say is true.

Fuck.

He's insane.

"Mom said you were engaged to a," Carter pauses, making air quotes, "'blue collar man.' Someone beneath your station and rank in life. She contacted me, asked me to keep an eye on you, and make you uncomfortable."

Mom? My *mother?*

"What?" I whisper. "Make me... uncomfortable?"

He half-shrugs a shoulder. "She seemed to think that if I somehow pitted you against your fiancé, that Judson could move in."

"Mom... what? This makes no sense."

Judson smirks in a way that makes my toes curl. "It makes perfect sense, Beatrice. She wants you with me, because joining our families means uniting two of the most lucrative companies in America. It's why they wanted us together to begin with. You were the one that decided to fuck things up. And now it's my job to make things work again. To keep peace in the family, if you will."

"By kidnapping me," I whisper. "And forcing me to—what?"

His eyes darken. "Marry me," he says.

I get to my feet but he's too fast, his hand on the gun, and a shot rings out like thunder. I scream, my ears ringing, as glass shatters and the lights dim. He's shot the chandelier. Holy shit. The man is out of his fucking mind.

I swallow and try to get my bearings. "And what the hell do *you* have to do with all this, Carter?"

Carter looks away, frowning.

"He needed money," Judson says. "Hard to keep a heroin habit going when mommy and daddy weren't doing handouts anymore. She decided she'd get him to do her dirty work by giving him money. Only I offered far more than she did."

"I see," I say, swallowing the lump in my throat. He's betrayed me. He's kidnapped me and brought me to this psychopath for money. I stare at Judson, willing myself to stay calm. "So what I'm supposed to do is pretend that somehow, magically, this is alright. That you haven't kidnapped me. And then... what? Go off and marry you and we live happily ever after?"

The grin dims on Judson's face. "You think I'm stupid, don't you?" he asks. I suddenly realize I've made a terrible mistake. He's out of his mind, and I'm stirring the hornet's nest. He gets to his feet, eyes cold with fury. "No. You'll announce that you've broken off your engagement with Officer Williams. You'll cut ties with whatever losers you've befriended in the city, and you'll come with me. We'll go to your parents and announce our engagement. And then you'll play nice."

"Why?" I whisper.

He stalks to me and I try to pull away but there's nowhere to go. He gets so close to me I can smell stale whiskey and the scent of his overpowering, expensive cologne. My stomach roils as he reaches for both my wrists and pins them to my sides. "I can make it worth your while," he whispers. "You like pain? I can work with that, sweetheart." Little hairs on my neck stand on end, my skin prickling as if pelted with tiny bits of hail, cold and shocking. I shiver at his touch, and I'm blinded with the need to escape, to get out of here, *to get to Zack.* Without thinking, I yank my knee up. Just in time, he blocks the blow, rears back, and smacks the side of my head with the butt of his gun. I scream at the sound of a second gunshot, dizzy from the blow, and hear a second, dismal, manly scream.

I gasp at the sight of a pool of blood on the ground, Carter grabbing at his side.

"You shot him," I whisper.

"You bitch," Judson growls, pushing me down on the couch. "You like to be put in your place? I'll put you in your fucking place." He punches the side of my face again, and the taste of wet metal explodes in my mouth. I whimper at a third and fourth blow. I'm losing consciousness, my head spinning as if I'm twirling on a merry-go-round. I bring my arms up instinctively to block the blows, as he hits me again and again until I can hardly move from the dull pain. He pushes me down and he's on top of me, his weight oppressive and sickening. I'm dimly aware of the whir of a zipper.

"You bitch," he growls. "I'll show you who you fucking belong to." I realize with a shocking stab of fear that he's going to take me, rape me, *destroy* me.

I'll kill him first.

I scream like a rabid animal as he tears at my clothes, fabric ripping with finality, when a sound I can't quite identify makes Judson sit up and whip his head around. He reaches for his gun at the sound of pounding feet and shouts coming our way.

"In here!" shouts Carter, still conscious in his blood on the floor, screaming for someone to get us. I shove Judson, but when he tumbles, he takes me with him. We fall to the floor and my vision blurs as my head strikes concrete. Then he's lifted off me and a dull sound of flesh hitting flesh assaults me. I curl into a ball and duck my head, trying to keep myself safe.

"I'll fucking kill him." I know that voice. I blink and look up the furious face of Zack. He has Judson by the arms and he lifts him just high enough to knee him then drop him on the floor. Armed, uniformed officers surround us, but I'm no longer aware of anything after I see Judson cuffed, because now Zack has me. *He has me.*

"You came for me," I say, as he lifts me straight up into his arms and away from the crowd of people who've infiltrated this small room. "How did you find me? How did you know?"

"Shhh, baby," he says, holding me tight. "There will be time for talking later. Not now, doll. Let's get you safe and better." He kneels, me still in his arms, and cradles me on his lap. Cupping my chin in his hand, he lifts my eyes to his, the warm depth of chocolate brown eyes meeting mine with tenderness and sadness as his gaze sweeps over my bruised and broken face. "You're safe now, Beatrice." He brushes back a strand of hair, leans down, and tenderly kisses the apple of my cheek, then brushes his lips against mine. I taste salt and metal, my tears and blood intermingling in the kiss that brings us back together. "You're safe now," he repeats. Closing my eyes, I lean my head on his chest, and begin to cry.

━━━

"AND WHEN SHE told me how to find your brother, it was an easy matter to track where they'd been. The man I had on you? He caught the plate and tailed you all the way here. We lost the connection and I thought he was compromised, but he had enough to go on and called it in. He wouldn't go in without backup on my orders, but as soon as we arrived, we swarmed the place."

We're sitting at a small, circular table at the hospital. There's a little café with coffee and tea after hours. Carter is being observed upstairs. He's sustained injuries and significant blood loss, but he's fine. I'm happy to hear that. Zack doesn't give a shit.

"Officer Williams?" A young man with a shock of red hair and pale skin tips his head into the doorway. "Mr. and Mrs. Moore have arrived to see Carter." Zack gets to his feet and takes my hand, just as my mother and father come running inside.

"Where is he?" My mother seems to think causing a scene is the best way to get sympathy, as she demands to know Carter's whereabouts at the front desk.

"Mr. and Mrs. Moore."

Zack's eyes are hard as flint, his voice sharp, as he gets their attention. It was only by pulling strings Zack was able to tend to my injuries himself, and forbid my being admitted. My parents spin around and look at us, my mother's eyes narrowing at the sight of Zack holding my hand. My father, however, rushes to me.

"Beatrice," he murmurs. "Are you okay?"

I nod, but I step back and let Zack do his thing. I trust

him to do what needs to be done. He was right. And now he's going to see that justice is served.

"Yes, sir, Beatrice is fine. I am, however, going to have to order your wife brought into custody and questioned."

"That's ridiculous," my mother sputters.

Now, I speak up.

"It is *not.*" I look at my father when I speak. "Carter had me kidnapped at Judson's command. By their admission, mom put him up to this. She had Carter stalk me to make me uneasy and break up with Zack. *She* is the one who started all this. I don't even want to look at her."

"Beatrice!" Her voice is pleading, and when I look to her for the first time ever I see how wan her face is, the liver spots on her hands pronounced against pale, thin skin.

My father looks from me to Zack, then nods slowly. "You rescued her?" he asks.

Zack pulls me tighter against him. "Yes, sir."

"Thank you," he says. Then he takes a step back from mom. "Do what you need to, officer."

Chapter 18

I'm pulled from sleep suddenly, sitting straight up in bed, and quickly assessing what woke me. Beatrice is tangled in the sheets, thrashing, her eyes still closed.

"Baby," I say, wrapping my strong arms around her to stop the flailing limbs. She continues to writhe, harder now, so I sharpen my voice to get her attention. "*Beatrice. Stop.*" She freezes, trained to obey that tone, and her lids flutter open, blue pools of fear, until she meets my gaze. Then her brow softens, and she drops her head to my chest.

"Zack," she breathes. "Thank God you're here." Poor thing's still shaken from what happened and hell, I don't blame her. I want to drag the men responsible out of jail and beat them senseless.

We lay in the silence. Her heart thumps like the beating of a drum against my bare chest. I hold her tight until her breathing slows and I think she's fallen back asleep. But then she reaches out for my face and runs her palm along the scruff of my beard. She needs to be sure of me. I close my eyes, inhale, and hold her even tighter. I'm not a praying man but in this moment, I give thanks for the warmth of her skin flush against mine, the sweet smell of lilacs in her hair, and the sound of her breathing returning to normal.

Until I thought I lost her, I'd made up my mind. I was a dominant, through and through, and I'd never be with a woman who couldn't be my submissive. I never have and never would. But here, in the dark, holding her close like this, I realize I was wrong. I could give it up for her. I love her.

We'd decided it best not to talk things over tonight, not when the pain of everything is still so raw. I checked her wounds and helped her strip out of her clothes to take a shower. I'd scrubbed her myself, soft and slow and gentle, until her shoulders drooped with exhaustion, then I towel-dried her off, brushed her hair, and tucked her into bed. My heart was full.

What I wanted was a woman to take care of. Beatrice gave that to me.

"I was wrong, Zack," she whispers, trailing her hand down the side of my face to my shoulder, her small hand tucked into the hollow of my neck.

"We don't need to talk about this now, doll," I begin.

"Please, sir."

Sir?

"You don't have to do this, Beatrice," I say as gently as I can. "I don't have to be your sir. I can just be… your man. Just Zack."

She shakes her head on my chest and lifts her face, her eyes vivid with unshed tears. "But I want this. I want you. I want all of it."

I push the hair out of her eyes and tuck it behind her head, still slightly damp, then gently smooth my thumb over the purplish bruise on her cheek.

"I could kill him," I whisper. "I could fucking kill him

for laying hands on you. He ever touches you again, I'll break every one of his fingers, one by one."

She swallows, her whisper matching mine as she responds. "I know."

Another beat passes in silence as she slowly turns herself so she's resting her chin on her hand and looking up at me.

"You are so fucking beautiful," I say, my voice thick with emotion. "And so brave, baby."

"Do you really think so?" There's a desperation I've never heard in her voice.

"God, yes," I say, nodding. I draw my fingers through her hair and her lids flutter shut, as I gently knead my fingers along the back of her neck. "You were raised with money, baby, but handicaps. And you've overcome that. You've made a life for yourself, and you've done it well. You have jobs you do. You have friends who love you." I smile at her and tweak her nose. "A boyfriend who loves you." Her eyes flutter open.

"Don't you mean a dom?" she asks softly, then bites her lip. There's a question in her eyes. Does she want me to be her dom? I won't push it. But hell, I want to give her what she needs.

"That's up to you. You need to know I'm sorry," I say. "I fucked up, baby. I never should've done what I did without telling you. It was wrong of me and I need to apologize."

She nods. "You were right, though. I needed someone to watch me. Those guys were *sick* and if you'd told me you had someone watching me, I'd have flipped my lid." She frowns. "Okay so I kinda *did*."

I can't help but chuckle. I clip her gently under the chin. "You're so damn cute."

She sighs, turns her head, and rests her cheek against

my chest. I hold her there, just listening to her breathing. I softly rub her back, feeling the warm, supple skin beneath my hands.

Earlier today, I thought she was lost. And now she's mine again. I'll move heaven and earth to keep it that way.

"So brave," I whisper. "And so strong."

"That's what I was afraid of, you know," she says. "I was afraid that if I submitted to you that I was somehow *weak*. Dependent on you. Unable to take care of myself, you know?"

"Mhm."

"You know, Diana set me straight earlier."

I bite back a smile. I had a feeling she would. I'll buy Diana the best damn wedding gift money can buy. "Oh?"

"She told me that what was really holding me back wasn't anything but *fear*. You know? And she was right. God, she was so right. I was afraid that submitting to you meant I was somehow weaker. Not strong."

"Hell, baby, it takes incredible strength to submit. You think *I'd* have the balls to kneel before someone and grant them authority? Hell *no.*"

She giggles, the sound musical and fucking adorable. "It's *not* easy."

"It's not easy, and it's not a sign of weakness. You willingly give me that submission, doll. That takes *strength*. And it's *beautiful.*"

"Thank you."

I listen to her heart beating with mine, and I know I want this forever. Always.

"Diana was right, Zack," Beatrice says, her voice stronger now. "When she said I was afraid. And God, Zack. It's true." She swallows. "She says when I face my fears, I build trust with you."

"When *we* do," I say, squeezing her hand by my side.

She sighs in contentment and turns to face me. "Yes, sir. I love you."

I reach down and kiss her forehead. "And I love you." I tug a lock of her golden hair. "Does that mean I still get to spank that ass?"

She grins at me, a flash of pearly white in the darkness. "I wouldn't have it any other way."

Epilogue

Two months later

"YOU DID *NOT,*" Diana says, holding Beatrice's manicured hand in hers, her jaw dropping at the band that wasn't there the day before. Beatrice was adamant. Every woman she knew growing up valued the size and worth of the diamond on their fingers, and she said she refused to get one. She wanted nothing but a simple wedding band in rose gold. It worked for me. The band was only part of what I had planned for her.

"You always were one competitive son of a bitch," Tobias says with a chuckle, punching my shoulder.

"Damn right," I say, watching as Diana yanks Beatrice over to her and gives her a hug so tight it leaves Beatrice breathless. "Couldn't let you be the first, man."

Diana's wearing her wedding gown and she's just said her vows to Tobias. We're on our way to the reception hall to take pictures and shit, but Beatrice had something to tell

Diana. We eloped in a quiet ceremony, just the two of us and a Justice of the Peace in the heart of NYC. She's told no one yet. My parents were a bit bemused but happy for me when I called them. Next summer, I'll take her to the Cape and to the beach and introduce her to my parents. She'll love them.

Her parents will find out when she's good and ready.

"You did the right thing, man," Tobias says, watching our girls hug each other. Beatrice didn't need a big wedding. She needs me. Just like I need her.

I nod. He's right. It was the right thing.

But I have one more thing to do.

———

"YOU'RE QUIET, ZACK," Beatrice says, reaching for my hand across the console as I make my way back to my place. We've just had one hell of a session at Verge, and I'm still pumped, but there's another reason my heart is beating rapidly and my pulse quickening. I squeeze her hand, then release it, gently grazing the pads of my thumbs over the slightly raised rope marks around her wrists. The pattern is beautiful, a physical symbol of her trust.

Tonight, we take it to the next level. We've talked about this, and though she's on board and knows what's coming, I'm still not sure how this will all play out. We stand at the very precipice of taking our relationship to the next level.

"Yeah, baby," I say finally. "A little quiet. Just a lot on my mind, doll, and none of it's bad."

She nods, resting her hand on the console and allowing me to finger her wrist, feel her pulse, her skin as soft as silk. Sometimes I need to be quiet, and she knows that about me. Hell, it's one of the reasons I know we're meant for each other. My job is to help her reach her full potential, to support her, and take care of her the best I can. And she takes care of me. Just because I'm the dom doesn't mean that I don't need her every bit as much as she needs me. She fulfills my need to protect, but supports me as I am, no judgment. And it's in that mutual give and take that we find our fulfillment.

It's why I've planned what I'm about to do tonight. Why what we do next needs to happen.

After we reach our place and park the car, I take her by the hand and lead her upstairs, pulling her a little closer to me as the chill autumn wind picks up, making her shiver. I instinctively tuck her against my side, shielding her from the cold. She leans into me, accepting my protection in quiet thanks.

Jesus, she's mine. My wife. And I'll never fucking take that for granted.

She's quiet, maybe in deference for my own need for contemplation, or perhaps she intuits that tonight is a special night. Whatever the reason, though, I can't help but pull her into the entryway to my building, lightly push her up against the wall, pull her head back and claim her mouth in a hard kiss that makes her knees buckle. "I love you," I say in a vehement whisper that brings tears to her baby blues, her eyes like the ocean at sunrise, filled with hope and light and the promise of good things to come.

She swallows hard, reaches a hand to my cheek and gently cups my jaw. "And I love you."

Our lives are about to change, and we both know this. There's no going back to the way things were. Tonight, and tomorrow, and the days and weeks and years after that, we face as one. In silence, we make our way upstairs.

It's been a long few weeks, and we're both tired. The night isn't over yet, though.

"Go get yourself ready for bed," I order, slipping her jacket off her shoulders. I give her a playful smack on the ass, sending her to go do as she's been told. Squealing, she goes, and as soon as the bedroom door closes, I get ready to meet her. I want this to be as perfect as she is.

I strike a match, the scent of smoke filling my senses, then warm vanilla as the wick burns the ivory wax. I stare at the candle, the flickers almost hypnotic. Will I remember the details of this night even when I'm old?

I'm listening to the sound of running water in the bathroom. She's been living with me now long enough I know her routine. She'll wash her face and remove her makeup, then slather some cream on, before she brushes and flosses her teeth. When I hear the final turn of the faucet handle, I'll know she's finishing up and about to join me. When the faucet squeaks off, I grab the square-shaped box from the bedside table and lay it next to me on the bed, where she can't see it.

The door to the bathroom opens, and my heart melts a little at the sight of her in a pair of sheer red boxers and a tiny white cami, her hair wild and crazy, tied up in a little knot thing on the top of her head. She wears no jewelry or makeup, and she's never looked so beautiful.

"Zack?" she asks, tipping her head to the side. "Everything okay, sir?"

A flare of pleasure floods me at the *sir*. A reminder that she's my submissive and I'm her dominant. It comes naturally to her now, but I know it hasn't always. Knowing she chooses this is what makes it so special.

I fought for her. And hell, I won.

"Everything's more than okay, doll," I say, my voice

gentle at first, but now she needs to know I'm serious. I point to the floor between my knees. "Kneel, please."

She's tired but curious, her eyes expectant, never leaving mine as she takes her position kneeling before me, gently resting her hands on my knees. I take in a deep, cleansing breath to steady my nerves, no sound in the room now but her breathing.

"We talked about this," I say, before swallowing, "And I know this is what you want. But you tell me now if you're at all hesitant with what I'm about to do." She sobers a bit, a little knot forming between her brows, but she says nothing, just watches as I lift the gleaming black box. Then her eyes go wide and her mouth parts open when I lift the lid. There, nestled against soft folds of velvet, lays the collar I've had hand-crafted for her.

I lift the collar before placing the box back on the bed. It's a sturdy chain, rose gold in color with tiny, intricate engraving along the chain, two waves of lines woven into one beautiful pattern. "Do you see this?" I ask. "There are two waves that interlock to form a pattern. Neither is thicker or more pronounced than the other, and together they form a beautiful pattern they wouldn't if separated."

"Like us," she whispers. I nod, my left hand brushing her cheek in praise.

"Yeah, baby. And I chose the rose gold because it fits you. Beautiful, feminine, and the strongest gold there is." It also matches her wedding band, and it cost a fucking mint, but she doesn't need to know that. She's worth it.

"It's discreet," I continue, "with a tiny lock in the back. It has one key, and that will stay with me."

She swallows, her eyes now on the collar in my hand.

"Are you ready, Beatrice?"

"Yes. Please, sir," she says, her voice teeming with

emotion. She closes her eyes and lifts her chin, baring her neck to me, and I'm filled with the knowledge that she trusts me. Earning this woman's trust is the single most important accomplishment of my whole damn life. I'll always, always honor that.

I take a deep breath, steadying my hands that want to shake, before I slide the collar around her neck. The pink-tinged gold lays against her creamy skin and looks as if it was made for her. "I love you," I whisper, as I turn the clasp. Once it's fastened, it will lock.

"And I love you," she whispers at the same time the soft *click* tells us she's collared.

"Come here," I say, the need to claim her, to seal this moment making me near primal with need. I lift under her arms, pull her right up off the floor, raking down the red boxers and baring her to me. I take just a moment to seal this night with a kiss, before I'm removing my own clothes. I need to take her.

"Sir," she whispers, fingering the gold chain at her neck. She's wiping away tears and reaching for me, wrapping her arms around my neck, lifting her body to mine. Her knees part and she welcomes me, arching her back but saying nothing as I slide into her with a groan.

"You're mine," I say with a firm thrust.

"Yours," she whispers.

The light of the candle flickers and she closes her eyes, welcoming the connection of heart, body, and mind. "I love you," she says, her voice thick with emotion. And as her body tenses on the verge of climax right before I claim my own orgasm, I breathe with her as I make a promise. "I love you. I'll say it when you wake up and when you go to sleep, whisper it in your ear and proclaim it from the rooftops. You're mine today, and always will be."

"And you're mine," she says, her eyes twinkling in that way I adore.

I'll never fully tame this woman. She's a wild one, and always will be. But she's *my* wild one.

THE END

Chapter one from Deliverance *(an NYC Doms standalone novel)*

"You son of a bitch," I hiss, intentionally keeping my voice low. Crazy, half-cocked, vindictive ex-lover isn't normally my thing.

Hell, there's a first for everything, though.

"Diana! *Stop.* This is stupid, and girl, you *know* I know stupid when I see it because I've done *all the stupid* in my life." Beatrice pleads with me to think twice as she shuffles toward me, trying to place her small frame between me and the car I'm about to destroy.

"Stop the lecture." My hands tremble as I hold the keys, glaring past my blonde-haired, blue-eyed bestie, and focusing my hatred on the silver Maserati. I march past Beatrice, and before I can change my mind, dig the tip of my key into the gleaming exterior with maniacal glee. Crouching down, I take grim pleasure in destroying the most beautiful car I've ever looked at. Sat in. Been fucked in.

"Did you tell Little Miss High and Tight your sob story?" I cackle to the car as if it's my ex-boyfriend embodied. I'd only just met the guy a few weeks ago, my first real boyfriend since my ex-husband took off, but I'd managed to convince myself he was *the one*. My savior. My hero. With a particularly vicious swipe, I lose my footing and nearly sprawl onto the snowy sidewalk, but I catch myself on the bumper. Wind whips at my hair, icy snow lashing my bare skin, but I hardly feel it.

Tequila for the win.

"Diana," Beatrice cajoles. "You've had too much to

drink. God, woman! Get ahold of yourself! You've done it, okay? You've done enough. I shouldn't have let you out of the car. This isn't *you*. You're too smart to pull this teenaged shit. Just get in the car and I'll——"

"Leave me alone." I love this girl to death, but I don't trust myself not to shove her out of my way if she tries to stop me. I scrape the key once more, so deep it feels like fucking nails on a chalkboard, but I like knowing the damage will be severe. "You don't know what it's like to walk into your bedroom and see some bitch with her lips wrapped around your boyfriend's cock."

Scrraaape.

"You don't know what it's like to see betrayal in the eyes of the man who said he loved you."

Scraaaape.

"You don't know what it's like," my voice catches on a dry sob, so I underscore my angst with another cut of the key, "to have to explain to your son that the bastard who promised to take him to the drive-in movie theater was a lying piece of shit who'll never come back."

Scrape, scrape, scraaape.

Sitting back on my heels, I eye the destruction with triumph.

Beatrice talks to me like one might speak to a rabid animal, her hands outstretched in a gesture meant to calm. "I may not know those things, but I do know that——" She freezes, her voice now panicked. "Oh. Oh, *shit*. Diana, stop. Oh my *God*. We have to go."

But before I can respond, the deep growl of a man's voice right behind me—a voice *I do not know*—makes me nearly stumble.

"What the *fuck* are you doing to my car?"

Shit.

His... car?

I turn, my cheeks hot despite the freezing cold, to stare into the terrifyingly furious face of the biggest man I've ever seen. He towers over me, even wearing my tallest spiky heels, and the involuntary step I take back helps me see him better. Everything about him is dark, with his swarthy skin and nearly-black hair, but it's his eyes—black as coal beneath thick, heavy brows, that pin me in place. I can't move. I can't speak. I can barely think.

His jaw, covered in thick, dark stubble, tightens when his huge, muscled arms cross his expansive chest.

In any other time or place, I'd find the man sexy as fuck. But now?

"Your car?" I whisper.

"My car," he says in a low growl. "What are you doing to *my* fucking car?"

I blow out a breath and close my eyes.

I'm screwed.

Deliverance *is now live in the Amazon store.*

Look for Conviction, *a standalone entry in the NYC Doms series, out June of 2018.*

About the Author

USA Today bestselling author Jane Henry pens stern but loving alpha heroes, feisty heroines, and emotion-driven happily-ever-afters. She writes what she loves to read: kink with a tender touch. Jane is a hopeless romantic who lives on the East Coast with a houseful of children and her very own Prince Charming.

Sign up for Jane's newsletter, and get a free read! Sign up *HERE*.

Have you joined my Facebook reader group? We have exclusive giveaways, cover reveals, Advanced Reader Copies, and visits from your favorite authors. Come on over and join in the fun! Join the Club!

Stay in touch with Jane!

www.janehenryromance.com
janehenryromance@gmail.com

Other titles by Jane you may enjoy:

NYC Doms

Deliverance

Contemporary fiction

The Billionaire Daddies Trilogy

Beauty's Daddy: A Beauty and the Beast Adult Fairy Tale
Mafia Daddy: A Cinderella Adult Fairy Tale
Dungeon Daddy: A Rapunzel Adult Fairy Tale

The Boston Doms

My Dom (Boston Doms Book 1)
His Submissive (Boston Doms Book 2)
Her Protector (Boston Doms Book 3)
His Babygirl (Boston Doms Book 4)
His Lady (Boston Doms Book 5)

Her Hero (Boston Doms Book 6)

My Redemption (Boston Doms Book 7)

Begin Again (Bound to You Book 1)

Come Back to Me (Bound to You Book 2)

Complete Me (Bound To You Book 3)

Bound to You (Boxed Set)

Black Light: Roulette Redux

Sunstrokes: Four Hot Tales of Punishment and Pleasure
(Anthology)

A Thousand Yesses

Westerns

Her Outlaw Daddy

Claimed on the Frontier

Surrendered on the Frontier

Cowboy Daddies: Two Western Romances

Science Fiction

Made in the USA
Monee, IL
28 July 2020

37151365R10115